Coyote in Provence

By

Dianne Harman

Published by: Dianne Harman
www.dianneharman.com

Interior design and typesetting by
Taylor Page Designs
taylorpagedesigns.wordpress.com

Cover design by
MAE I DESIGN
www.maeidesign.com

ISBN: 978-0-9889349-2-4

DEDICATION

To my friend Jackie, who convinced me that readers wanted to know what happened to Maria after they finished reading *Blue Coyote Motel*.

"Coyotes, by nature, typically avoid human contact."

Warner Johnston

PART ONE

PROVENCE, FRANCE   AUGUST, 2010

CHAPTER 1

Since arriving in Provence several months earlier, Elena had avoided contact with people, afraid that someone would discover her secret. She kept to herself, figuring the less people knew about her, the better off she'd be. Every day she lived in fear that the California police authorities would come knocking on her door. She hadn't made any effort to become friendly with the village women, and as a result, developed a reputation for being aloof. In turn, no one tried to make friends with her. By her own choice, she had become something of a recluse and a loner, living in her small cottage near the village of St. Victor la Coste.

Elena was vaguely aware that her presence in the small village had been the subject of conversations by the local residents. Like all villages around the world, gossip trumped fact. The inhabitants were always hungry for tidbits of information, particularly if it involved a beautiful rich American widow.

From time to time she wondered what she would do for the rest of her life now that she was living in Provence. She pushed those thoughts aside while she struggled with the symptoms of withdrawal from the drug known as Freedom.

She'd grown reliant on the drug and without it, she was experiencing bouts of depression. She felt lost and worthless as she tried to get the last of it out of her system.

Then there was the problem of no longer having access to the anti-aging hormone. Elena couldn't help it. Every time she passed a mirror, she was compelled to look into it and see if she could see any signs of aging. When her husband Jeffrey died, so did the formulas for Freedom and the anti-aging hormone he'd been injecting her with for several years.

Lately she'd been having nightmares about Jeffrey. She'd wake up in the middle of the night, sweating, her heart beating, reliving that fateful afternoon in his secret lab at the Blue Coyote Motel, when her life had changed forever. Maybe it was time to find something to do, something to take her mind off of the past.

There's not a weed left in the garden, the cottage is spotless, and I can't continue cooking this much food just for myself. Hate to admit it, but I'm not only lonely, I'm bored. Maybe I should get a job. I don't need the money, but it would give me something to do. I wonder if Henri's Bakery needs some help. Maybe he'd even hire me as a cook.

Five minutes later, after a short walk from her cottage to the village, she opened the door of the bakery and smelled the pleasant aromas of yeast, baking bread, and gently simmering soups. It was 10:30 in the morning and the bakery was empty. The early morning croissant crowd had already come and gone and the lunch crowd had yet to arrive.

St. Victor la Coste, where Elena settled after she left California, was in an area of Provence known for its food, wine

2

and art. Henri's Bakery had acquired a far-flung reputation for having superb food. Even though it was very small and not open for dinner, it had earned two Michelin stars. The bakery looked like something out of a travel magazine with small tables set with red and white checkered tablecloths, both inside and outside. Umbrellas covered the outdoor tables on the sidewalk and local wine flowed freely from the bottles on the tables.

During the summer months the village was crowded with tourists eager to eat, drink, and enjoy the local art. Several nearby older chateaus had been converted into bed and breakfasts with reservations required up to a year in advance. Although the village was about 150 miles from Marseille, many visitors felt the high quality of the food, combined with the outstanding work of numerous local artists, was worth the extra effort it took to travel to the area. The village had become a mecca for art lovers who were hungry and thirsty, and Henri's Bakery was at its heart.

There was one art gallery in the village and several more in nearby towns, all of which catered to the tourists. Elena imagined it had been much quieter before it had been discovered by the "in" crowd, but the villagers made sure it retained its charm. She felt she'd been very lucky when the rental agent had driven her to the cottage located close to the small and charming village.

"*Bon jour, Mademoiselle*," Henri said, greeting Elena as she stepped into the bakery. He was a walking advertisement for what the owner of a French bakery should look like. His hair was covered with specks of flour and his arms were thick and muscular from years of rolling out dough. Henri was a master baker, and his large belly indicated he also had a taste for his own food.

COYOTE IN PROVENCE

"*Monsieur,* although we've spoken to one another several times, we've never been introduced. I am Elena Johnson. I live in a small cottage just outside the village. I like to cook and I'm pretty good at it. I wonder if you could use some help in your kitchen for a few hours, maybe before and during lunch. I thought I might make some soups and casseroles. My husband and I used to own a motel in California where I made meals for the guests, although it wasn't a true restaurant."

Over the months, Elena had noticed that Henri had two other people assisting him with the baking as well as an ever-changing group of young people who worked as the wait staff. Summers were very busy with the large crowds of international visitors who always seemed to find their way to Henri's Bakery.

"*Mademoiselle,* pardon me, but I have heard you don't need to work and that you inherited a great sum of money when your husband died."

"I see you've been listening to the local gossip, Henri. While it's true I don't need to work for money, I do need to work for me. My days are becoming too long, and I have too little to do. You always seem so busy and I know your true love is baking. If you hire me, you could spend more of your time doing that."

Elena was a very beautiful woman, a fact which had not escaped the town baker. Looking at her, he could feel his heart beat a little faster. She had deliberately gained weight after arriving in Provence to disguise herself, but even the additional twenty pounds couldn't detract from her beauty.

"What kind of wage would you expect to be paid, if I hired you? And before I hire you, if I do, I need to know if you really are a good cook. Why don't you bring me lunch tomorrow and we'll talk after that?"

"Thank you. I would expect to be paid whatever is fair, and I'll be here at 11:00 tomorrow morning with lunch. That will give you time to eat before the lunch crowd starts arriving, and you'll probably be through with most of your baking by then. See you tomorrow and thanks for considering me. *Bon jour.*"

Elena left the bakery and went to the small village grocery called *un épicier*, wondering what she could make for Henri that would make him want to hire her. Debating what to cook, she walked by the meat counter. There, between plump chickens and double-cut pork chops, was a row of beautifully arranged veal shanks.

Ahh! What man doesn't love braised veal shanks over rich, buttery noodles? Perfect. I'll get two veal shanks, and I already have the celery, carrots and onions. I've got fresh rosemary and thyme in my garden. I'll make a strawberry and spinach salad to serve with it. That will add color, and they're also in my garden. This will definitely work!

She rose early the following morning to get the rosemary, thyme, strawberries and spinach from her garden and spent the morning preparing the meal. At 10:50 she wrapped the plated veal shanks, noodles, and gravy with aluminum foil to keep them warm, transferred the chilled salad into a covered plastic container, and put it all into two small picnic hampers.

The meal wasn't the only thing she'd carefully arranged. Elena had learned long ago the effect her beauty had on men. She had no qualms about unbuttoning her blouse a tiny bit lower than discretion advised. She wore a white silk blouse which

5

clung to her ample breasts, along with a wide red belt encircling her waist over tight white silk slacks. She looked in the bathroom mirror and smiled approvingly.

As she walked down the lane to the bakery, she hoped Henri would like the lunch she had prepared for him. She also hoped his wandering eyes would approve of what she was wearing. She suspected they would.

"Bon jour, Henri. I've made a lunch for you of veal shanks with vegetables and gravy over noodles along with a nice strawberry and spinach salad. I didn't bring any bread. You're the master baker and your bread is far better than anything I can make. Would you like some wine to go with it? It's a warm day and a chilled rosé would be perfect."

"Let's go outside and eat," Henri said. He moved toward the bakery door. He wanted to be sure that the village men saw that the beautiful widow was having lunch with him.

Henri was having a difficult time deciding whether he should continue looking at Elena or try the veal shanks she had made for him. The food won. He took one bite of a veal shank and knew he was going to hire her. It was not only superb, it was much better than any he'd ever made.

"Elena, this is wonderful. It's the tenderest veal I've ever had. Please, share your cooking secret with me."

"Actually, Henri, it's a trick my mother taught me many years ago. I always brine white meat in buttermilk with some herbs and salt and pepper. I brined it for several hours yesterday afternoon, patted it dry, and put it uncovered in the refrigerator overnight. When I bake it, the skin crisps, but the inside stays moist. I'm so glad it pleases you."

"Elena, I know you like buttered croissants, but that's about it. If you care to tell me, I'd like to know more about you," Henri said, looking up as he continued to eat.

"It's no secret. My husband died after a long illness, and I needed to get away. I'd always read wonderful things about the Provence area of France and I thought I would see if they were true. I contacted a realtor when I got to Marseille and she showed me the small cottage just outside the village, where I'm living. I've come to love it here, but now I'm ready to do something. I would very much like to work here at the bakery. I hope you will have me," she said, smiling as she leaned slightly forward over the table in order to give Henri a better opportunity to admire her cleavage.

"When can you start? By the way, this meal is wonderful. You're a very good cook. As you know, I like to frequently change what I serve so it reflects the freshness of the seasons. Have you ever worked in a restaurant?"

"I can start tomorrow if you'd like. And no, although I've cooked a lot, I've never done it for large crowds like you have at lunchtime. What should I start with?"

"I think you should begin with a main dish, something like this, and a salad. You can fix whatever is in season, but I would like to see a variety of things. Be creative. Let's see what you come up with."

"Where will I get the ingredients? Do I order them, or do I buy them at the *épicier*?"

"I order food for the kitchen several times a week. In fact, Jacques, the man who provides my groceries, should be here soon. Why don't you begin in three days? You can talk to Jacques and think about what you'd like to start with, then place your order with him. He's very good at suggesting things that are in season. Ah, here he is now."

He waved to a fair-haired bearded man who was approaching their table. "Jacques, come, I want you to meet my new assistant chef, Elena Johnson." He poured Jacques a glass of rosé from the large bottle in the center of the table.

Jacques and Elena spent the better part of an hour deciding what she would need, and what dishes she should make for the coming week. While they were talking, the tables began to fill up and soon it was time for Henri to go back to his usual place behind the glass display shelves.

Elena walked back to her cottage, excited, and for the first time in months, looking forward to the future.

SEPTEMBER, 2010

CHAPTER 2

Jordan woke up rested after a good night's sleep with almost no jet lag. He wondered what the day would bring. Hopefully, it would be a repeat of last night: more great food, wine, and art.

Why hasn't Provence been on my list of "must visits?" What a fool I was not to have come here when I was a student at the Cordon Bleu, but it's just gone to the top of the list of places where I need to spend more time!

The breakfast Madame Pascal, the owner of the chateau, had told him about when he arrived the night before was even better than she'd promised. Promptly served at 9:00 a.m., there were muffins, fresh eggs gathered within the hour, fruit from the chateau's orchard, and European-style cured bacon. It was absolutely one of the best breakfasts he'd ever eaten. Just as he was finishing, Marc, the bellman/handyman who worked at the chateau, arrived and told him his rental car had been delivered.

"Thank you Marc," he said walking to the front door. "Do I need to take the driver somewhere?"

"No, I will drive him to the village. The rental agency from Marseille has a driver and car there to take him back. Here are the keys. He said you can return it either in the village or in Marseille, whichever you prefer."

Jordan opened the door leading to the circular driveway and was taken aback by the sleek silver Renault two-door parked there. *Wow, I'll be driving, eating and looking at art in style!*

By the time he showered and got dressed, it was eleven in the morning, meaning he had an hour before the shops closed for lunch. The time had come for him to look at the Alfred Mitchell painting he'd traveled so far to see. If the painting Lydia and Sam Martin had seen in the village was an original, it might be the painting that had been stolen from the Laguna Beach gallery. Knowing the Martins, Jordan was pretty sure the painting would be authentic.

He got in the Renault and listened with appreciation to the quiet purr of the engine when he turned the key in the ignition. He pulled out from the chateau's circular driveway and headed down the lane to the nearby village of St. Victor la Coste. Vineyards and olive trees lined the main road. Judging how heavy the vines were with grapes, he knew the annual wine crush would be starting soon.

Jordan parked just outside the village limits in a parking lot. The medieval streets in the village were too narrow for modern cars, and everyone walked or rode bicycles when they were in the village proper. He couldn't help but look around in amazement. It was a step back in time. The small streets were flanked by stone buildings, both residential and commercial, with tubs full of brightly colored flowers located next to almost every door. He easily found his way to the Galerie Reynaud on the Rue de la Republique.

As he approached the gallery, there in the window, just under the bright yellow canopy with the black letters, "Galerie Reynaud," was a painting attributed to Alfred Mitchell. Even from a distance, he knew it was an original. The artist was known for using dramatic contrasts and strong colors in his paintings of outdoor scenes. There was no mistaking it; the work had to be Mitchell's. A sign was posted on the door, "Closed for family business until 2:00."

Jordan looked up and down the street. It was after the tourist season and there were very few people on the streets of the small village. No one was paying attention to him. He slipped his smart phone out of its case and took a couple of quick photos of the painting. If it was the stolen one – which looked certain now – he needed to be very careful when he talked to the owner.

I wonder if the gallery owner has it on consignment or if he bought it, and if so, for how much, and from whom. I don't think the painting would be in the window if the owner knew it was stolen.

He walked around the village, admiring its quaintness and enjoying the diversion. In the middle of the village was a stone base with a plaque, honoring the men and women who served in World War II. Everywhere he turned, he was immersed in history; the charming buildings and streets had the settled look of having been there for several centuries. He thought how strange it was that in America you could see ads for antique televisions, as if there was such a thing. He remembered from his art classes that an antique had to be over one hundred years old before the term could properly be used. By any definition, the village definitely had an antique feel to it.

At the end of the street he saw a number of people sitting outside a building with the name "Henri's Bakery" on it. Jordan remembered reading about this particular bakery and that his

Michelin guidebook had given it two stars. Glancing at his watch, he saw it was lunch time.

Jordan walked down the street and sat down at one of the bakery's outdoor tables. The menu was written on a black chalkboard. The daily special, written in white chalk, was shrimp bisque with a shaved fennel and apple salad. Jordan had only been seated a few minutes when a lovely dark haired young woman brought him a plate of fresh bread and butter with a ramekin of Camargue salt.

"*Bon jour, Monsieur*," she said, "What may I bring you today?"

"How is the shrimp bisque? I rarely see it on a menu. I assume that the shrimp are fresh from the Marseilles area."

"Yes they are. People are raving about it and ordering seconds and thirds. I think we'll be out of it shortly."

"Really! Well then, I must try it."

"I'd be happy to get you a bowl. And may I suggest some rosé wine to go with it? It's a little warm today and the chilled rosé will go well with the bisque."

"Perfect. Yes, I'd like to order exactly what you suggested."

He buttered a piece of bread and slowly ate it as he took the picture of the Mitchell painting he had brought with him from California out of his pocket. He compared it to the photos displayed on his phone. There was no doubt in his mind - this was definitely the stolen painting.

Good God, that bread and butter may be the best I've ever had. He patted his lips with the napkin as the smiling waitress brought him another basket of bread.

So how does one smuggle a stolen painting into France? How does one sell it to a gallery owner without questions being raised? I can understand why the thief would try and sell it here, rather than in Paris where there would be far more knowledgeable collectors and gallery owners. I wonder if the gallery owner knew it was stolen, but decided no one in this small village would recognize that it was stolen.

He looked up and saw that the waitress was walking towards his table with his soup and salad. He stuck the picture back in his pocket. "*Merci bien*," he said. "I have a question. I like art and noticed a painting in the window of the art gallery down the street. Do you know anything about that particular painting?"

"*Non, Monsieur*. It's been there for several weeks. I walk by the gallery every day when I come to work, but I don't recognize the name of the artist whose work is currently on display in the window. I probably would know the name if he was from this region, since I've lived here all my life."

Jordan had taken several spoonfuls of the soup while the lovely waitress answered his questions regarding the gallery. "Thank you. I have another question for you. Would it be possible to meet the person who made this bisque? It's the best I've ever had. I'd like to compliment the chef."

"*Certainement*. Her name is Elena and I will tell her that you would like to speak with her. I'm sure she would like to hear your comments."

Just as Jordan was finishing his glass of rosé, one of the most beautiful women he had ever seen approached his table.

"*Monsieur,* I am Elena, the luncheon chef. You appear to be an American. I am too, so we can speak English to one another. My French is good, but I prefer to speak English."

She took a long look at Jordan as he stood up to greet her. He was about 6'2" and quite handsome, with a strong, physically fit appearance. His black hair was beginning to show a bit of grey at the temples, and intelligent, large brown eyes sparkled as he looked at her with appreciation.

"If you have a minute, would you sit down? I'm Jordan Kramer and your shrimp bisque is the best I've ever tasted. You are a master chef. I'm a gourmand, and eating is one of my hobbies. If I died today, I would die happy knowing that my last meal was your bisque."

"Please, don't do that. It could be very bad for business and Henri might fire me," she said laughingly as he pulled out a chair for her. "Tell me, what brings you to this small village?"

"Well, I could counter that by asking what brings a beautiful American woman who's a gifted chef to this small French village. How about if you tell me first, then I'll tell you?"

"It's no secret. I was widowed and decided to leave the United States. There were too many memories there." She paused, and smiled again. "I've been very happy here, particularly now that I am working at Henri's. I love to cook, but cooking for one is not very much fun. I much prefer hearing compliments from other people, rather than telling myself how good something tastes. Now it's your turn."

14

"I'm an art consultant. Some clients of mine asked me to come to this village and look at a painting they had seen in a local art gallery. As long as I was coming here, I decided to spend a few extra days and enjoy two of my other favorite things, food and wine. So far, I haven't been disappointed."

I don't want to alarm this beautiful lady by telling her the real reason I'm here. It's probably best to stick to my art consultant story as a cover. It wouldn't be the first time I've scared someone off when they found out I'm a police detective employed by the City of Los Angeles Police Department.

"That's interesting. I really don't know anything about art, but I like the painting in the front window of the gallery down the street. Uh-oh, I see that Henri is waving at me. I must go. Again, thank you for your compliment about my bisque," she said as she stood up.

"Elena, I've really enjoyed talking to you. I noticed that the restaurant isn't open in the evening. Would you care to join me for dinner tonight? I'd love to take you to one of your favorite restaurants."

"I wish I could help you, but since I've been here I've pretty much stayed in this village. However, if you like, you could come to my cottage this evening and I'll serve you something traditional from the area."

What am I thinking? I just asked some strange man to dinner. It's like someone else was speaking through my mouth. Well, now it's too late. I can't take back the invitation. Anyway, it's just for one night and after all, he is quite handsome.

"Thank you. I'd like that very much. I'll bring some wine and we'll have a good American conversation. What time should I plan on being there? And where is your cottage?

"Why don't you come at 7:00? Take the winding road on the east side of the village and go north. A few minutes after you leave the village, you'll see a stone fence with flowers growing on it. Look up to your right and there's a cottage with blue window frames. That's where I live. It's small, but it's perfect for me."

Elena gave him an encouraging smile and hurried back to the kitchen. A crisis was brewing. They had run out of the shrimp bisque and patrons were demanding more.

Jordan looked through the bakery window and followed her with his eyes as she hurried back to the kitchen. He definitely was looking forward to spending the evening with this beautiful woman.

CHAPTER 3

When she returned home from Henri's, Elena stood on the patio of her small stone cottage for a few minutes, looking at the village below. The view never failed to please her with its charming simplicity. She'd been in Provence for six months now and was finally beginning to feel comfortable. The numbing fear of being arrested and extradited to the United States was finally easing. She was certain the authorities knew she'd come to Marseille, but from there she'd been very careful not to leave a trail.

Elena had used her passport with her real name, "Maria Brooks," when she left the United States. Spending extra time in Phoenix and trying to find someone to sell her a false passport had not been an option. She'd been intent on one thing and one thing only, getting out of the country before she was detained as a suspect in the murder of her husband.

She remembered requesting a one-year residence card the day after she'd arrived in Marseille. She'd gone to the French Office of Immigration and Integration which was located several miles from her hotel in a very old government building. The man who authorized the card for her looked like he'd been there from the time it had been built.

"*Monsieur*, my name is Elena Johnson. All of my personal belongings were stolen during my flight from the United States to France. *S'il vous plait*, I need some identification. Can you help me?"

17

The French bureaucrat was far more interested in trying to look down her blouse than he was in her story, so when she left his office, she was officially Elena Johnson. For all intents and purposes, Maria Brooks no longer existed.

After she rented the cottage near the small village of St. Victor la Coste, she sent for funds from the secret Cayman Islands bank account she'd opened when Jeffrey, her husband, began to slide into madness. From time to time Elena had money transferred to the village bank in order to pay for her living expenses. She didn't want the townspeople to know how much money she had. Villagers could be nosy and talk was cheap. They didn't need to know that she had enough money to last a lifetime, maybe several.

As she thought about what to prepare for dinner, she still couldn't believe she'd asked a total stranger to her home. Elena promised herself she'd have one dinner with him and that would be the end of it.

CHAPTER 4

Jordan finished his wine, paid his bill, and wandered around the village until the gallery opened at 2:00 p.m. He wondered whether it would only be a matter of time until Western greed set in, and small villages like this one would no longer honor the tradition of closing for a leisurely lunch. Jordan loved being able to eat a big meal at lunchtime and then let it settle without having to immediately return to work.

When he entered Galerie Reynaud a small bell rang, letting the owner know that a customer had entered the shop. Jordan looked around and saw that the gallery had some very good art on display. Although most of it was contemporary, there was also some early 20th century art, mainly oils and a few watercolors. The landscape of the Provence area was prominent in a number of pieces, depicting rolling hills with picturesque vineyards and olive groves.

The paintings showed the seasons, and the various shades of colors created by the changing times of day. There were some still-life paintings and a few of the Marseille harbor. Most of them had Monsieur Reynaud's name on them. Looking at them, Jordan thought he was an extremely talented artist. Jordan didn't see any American paintings other than the one in the window.

While he was examining the art on the walls, a bearded bear of a man with a diamond stud in one ear pushed aside the draped doorway separating the gallery from his studio and walked over to Jordan.

"Bon jour, Monsieur. I am Alain Reynaud, the owner of this gallery. May I help you?"

He'd be perfect for a painting entitled "Portrait of an Artist," Jordan thought. The bear wore an open-necked man's renaissance shirt and jeans, covered by a paint-specked apron.

"Yes. I'm interested in the painting in the window."

"Ahh, that is a very good piece. I bought it from an American dealer. It's by Alfred Mitchell, a California artist. He was part of the California Impressionist movement of the early part of the 20th century. A number of American tourists have been interested in it. I am asking 4,500 euros for it."

"May I look at it? I have some other California artists in my collection, and I am always interested in adding to it."

"Oui. Let me get it out of the window for you."

Jordan spent several minutes inspecting the small painting which depicted a scene from the Sierra Nevada Mountains in California. The cliffs in the background were bathed in a pink light, with large boulders in the right foreground. The brilliant blues of the lake at the foot of the cliffs seemed to jump off the painting. There, at the very bottom of the painting, was the well-known signature, "Alfred Mitchell" in red block letters. A closer inspection only verified what Jordan had thought when he first saw it. It was an original, and it was the one that had been stolen from the gallery in Laguna Beach.

"Thank you. You have some very good pieces here and I particularly like your paintings. You're really able to transfer the beauty of the landscape of this area to the canvas. What led you to become an artist?"

"I can't remember a time when I didn't have a paintbrush in my hand. It's as if the brush was another finger. I planned on moving to Paris and living there after my studies at the Sorbonne, but I missed the countryside and came back here. I opened this gallery several years ago. Painting and art are my life."

Jordan thought back to his days when he studied to get his degree in art history. He'd known even then that he lacked the "hunger in the belly feeling" that creative artists like *Monsieur* Reynaud had to have to make painting their life. Many years ago he'd decided he'd appreciate their efforts instead of becoming an artist.

"I understand, my friend. I like the Mitchell painting a lot, but let me think about it. I'll be staying in the area for a few more days. Thank you for your time. I enjoyed talking to you," he said as he opened the gallery door to the cobblestone sidewalk.

Leaving the gallery, his thoughts turned to Elena and dinner. As a police detective, he was very wary of relationships, and unusually careful about the women he dated. He'd never been married or even lived with another woman. To Jordan, women were objects to be wined and dined and then taken to bed. For over twenty years, that had been his custom. None had complained, but none had ever convinced him there could be more to a relationship than wine, food and sex.

I can't believe I asked a woman I met on the patio of a bakery to dinner. I don't know anything about her other than

21

she's beautiful and she's a great cook. He smiled inwardly. *Well, I'm in France. Maybe it's something in the air that's causing me to act so rashly.*

He decided to buy a couple of bottles of wine for dinner from a winery he'd seen on his drive into the village that morning. Jordan drove to the winery and parked the Renault. He watched as people took what appeared to be large plastic jugs out of their cars and entered the door leading to the winery. He couldn't figure out what they were doing as he followed them into the building, curious.

Inside a large room in the winery were numerous tubes connected to large wine casks in the back of the building. People inserted the tubes into the plastic jugs and filled them with wine. There were some wine bottles on the shelves, but nothing like what was displayed in the Napa or Sonoma wineries. There was no tasting area, no sommelier, no cheese, crackers, or water, and no one explaining the different kinds of wines to the customers. People filled up their jugs, capped them, paid what seemed like ridiculously low amounts of money, and loaded them into the trunks of their cars. Jordan had traveled to a number of places in the world, but this method of selling wine was completely new to him.

"May I help you, *Monsieur?*" asked a rotund man with a flushed face.

"*Oui.* I'd like to buy two bottles of good red wine, and two bottles of good white wine. I didn't bring any containers with me. What do you suggest? I will be drinking the wine with an evening meal, but I don't know what the hostess is serving."

"*Certainement, Monsieur.* May I suggest a red Bandol and a white Sauvignon blanc? I think you'll be happy with both of them. Here, try a sip of each and see if you like them."

"Thank you," he said as he tried each of them. A moment later, he said, "Yes, those will be fine."

"Let me get them for you." He went into the back of the building and returned with a wine carrier. Jordan paid what he considered to be a shockingly low price and returned to his car, shaking his head. It was a far cry from what he would have paid in Napa.

He drove back to the chateau, deep in thought. As soon as he arrived, he dialed the number for the Laguna Beach, California chief of police. When the police department's operator answered, he said, "Chief Lewis, please. This is Detective Kramer. Yes, I'll wait until he finishes his call."

A few minutes later the chief's voice came on the line. "Well, Jordan, what have you found out?"

"The Mitchell is authentic and it definitely is the one that was stolen in the Laguna Beach heist. The gallery owner said he bought it from an American dealer. I don't think he knows it's stolen. How do you want me to proceed?"

"Since the Mitchell is there, and that area of Provence has become such a mecca for tourists, it would make sense if the man who sold it to the gallery owner sold the other stolen pieces to galleries located in the nearby area as well. That's assuming he's the thief."

"Chief, that's a large assumption. He may just be the middleman."

"That's true, but I think you should spend several days going to villages in the area that have art galleries, and see if any of the other stolen pieces are for sale. You have photographs of all of the pieces. Find out which villages have galleries and map out a route. Forget going to Paris. If the thief or some other person sold a painting to a gallery in a small village in the south of France, he's probably too smart to try and peddle any of them to galleries in Paris. He'd be worried about the authorities there alerting the galleries, and I think we can assume that buyers there are far more sophisticated."

"I can do that. How far south of Paris do you think I should start?" Jordan asked.

"I don't think you need to go farther north than Lyon. Give me a call or email me in a couple of days and let me know what you find out. Two questions stand out in my mind. Number one, is the guy who sold the Mitchell to the gallery the thief? And number two, if he is the thief, how did he get that much stolen art into France without raising red flags when he went through French Customs? It's not like you can put that much art in a suitcase and carry it on a plane."

As Jordan listened, he remembered having read about several well-known restaurants in the area around Lyon. He could combine his love of food with his search for the missing paintings. France was known for food and wine and with the addition of art, it was an irresistible combination.

"Maybe he has an accomplice in France," the chief went on to say. "Discretion is crucial. We don't want one of the gallery

24

owners blowing the whistle on you and making a potential suspect head for the hills. I know I don't need to tell you to be careful, Jordan, and to watch your back side. These pieces were stolen. Someone broke into the gallery. That same person does not want to be caught and you might be in danger. I assume you got the gun I arranged for delivery to you by the Marseille Police Department. Good luck!"

"Yes, Chief, I got the gun and I have it on me at all times. I agree. Violence is usually not far behind greed. I'll be very careful."

The last few days had been a whirlwind. Jordan thought back to the phone call that had started it all.

SOUTHERN CALIFORNIA

CHAPTER 5

Jordan's phone rang in police headquarters in downtown Los Angeles. "Art Theft Division. This is Detective Kramer."

"Hello Detective, I'm Chief Lewis. I run the Laguna Beach Police Department. Detective, do you remember the theft of several California Impressionist paintings that occurred at a gallery here in Laguna Beach a few months ago?"

"Sure. Everyone in the Southern California art world knows about that one. As I recall, there was a Payne, a Mitchell, a Rose, a Redmond, a Schuster and a Wendt, plus one other one. I think there were seven in all. Some of the best works from the California Impressionist period were stolen in that burglary."

"Yes, obviously you do remember."

Jordan continued, "The detective who initially investigated the case thought it might have been an inside job. I remember hearing that the thief used a glass cutter to cut a hole in the glass door next to the lock. The detective thought it must have been a woman, or a very small man, because the hole was so little, just large enough for someone with a very small hand to reach in and unlock the door. The alarm was connected to the door, but the thief was able to disarm it. Why do you ask?"

"Well, we've received a tip there's a Mitchell painting for sale in a small village located in the Provence region of France called St. Victor la Coste, about three hours north of

26

Marseille," Chief Lewis said. "A couple from Laguna Beach was on vacation in Provence. After lunch they were walking through the village when they happened on an art gallery, and much to their surprise, they saw an Alfred Mitchell oil painting prominently displayed in the window."

"That would be very unusual. Paintings by Mitchell are almost exclusively sold in the United States and mostly in California."

"Yes, they couldn't believe there would be an original Mitchell in the small village, but then they remembered there had been a burglary because it was in all the papers."

"Is this something I can help you with?" Jordan asked.

"Detective, I'd like you to go to France and help us investigate this lead. If you're agreeable, I'll call your captain and see if he'll loan you to our department for a few days. Yeah, I know, it's a tough gig, but someone has to do it. Actually, depending on what you find out, you might spend a few days there and look around the area to see if any of the other stolen paintings surface. What do you think?"

Are you kidding me? Provence is Mecca for a foodie like me and to have the police department pay for my trip? This just might be my lucky day!

"I think it would be fantastic. By the way, Chief, what's the name of the couple who saw the painting in Provence?"

"I think it's Martin or Mastin. I remember it started with an M. Why do you ask?"

27

"I have a side business advising art collectors on everything from authenticity to purchasing. Lydia and Sam Martin are California Impressionist art collectors who live in Laguna Beach. If it's them, you can be pretty sure that the Mitchell in the village is authentic. They're very sophisticated collectors."

"I checked the file while you were talking and yes, it was the Martins."

"Chief, when do you want me to go? Should I make my own reservations and turn them in for reimbursement, or will your department make them for me?"

"I want you to get there as soon as possible. I'm afraid someone else will recognize that piece and buy it. I understand that the gallery's asking price is much lower than what Mitchell's paintings command here in the United States. I'll have my administrative assistant make your flight arrangements and other travel details. I'd also feel better about this assignment if you were armed. I'll make sure the Marseille Police Department provides you with a gun."

"I'll start getting ready right now. Please give me your email address and your telephone number so I can get in touch with you as soon as I have any information."

Jordan wrote down the chief's email and phone number.

"Good luck and keep me posted." The chief sat back in his black leather swivel chair, pleased that Detective Jordan Kramer had agreed to go to Provence. Jordan was a legend in the art theft world. He'd solved cases ranging from stolen Tibetan artifacts to Picassos to Disney animation art. The Los Angeles

Police Department was very happy to have him as part of their Art Theft Division. The chief knew that Jordan had been on loan to a number of police departments throughout the United States helping them solve art theft cases that occurred in their jurisdiction.

I may just get lucky with him on this case. When the City Council votes on my next pay raise, I'd like it known that I was responsible for getting this case solved. Yeah, Jordan, good luck. I could use some too.

CHAPTER 6

The next two days were spent in a whirlwind of preparations. The chief's administrative assistant phoned Jordan and gave him the details about the travel arrangements she'd made for him. After getting his mail held, reserving space at the doggie hotel for his beloved black Labrador, Linus, and leaving a note for his cleaning lady, he found himself at the airport, suitcase in hand.

Jordan's Air France flight left on time. Luckily, it was a late afternoon flight. It would be almost twenty-four hours until he arrived in the little village of St. Victor la Coste. The flight to Paris, the layover on his way to Marseille, and the drive to the village all had to be figured into travel time. Fortunately his arrival at the chateau where he would be staying would be around dinner time, and he'd be able to go to bed immediately afterward. He planned to sleep on the plane.

He read the art magazines he'd brought with him and began the first of two novels that had been sitting on his nightstand for months. After a few hours he fell asleep, waking to the pilot's voice announcing that they were beginning their descent into Orly airport, just outside of Paris.

Jordan easily maneuvered his way through French Customs and Immigration, which took much less time than he thought it would. He had about an hour before his flight left for Marseille and he was hungry. At the airport news stand he bought Le Monde, the daily French newspaper, curious to see how much French he'd retained from the time he'd spent in France attending the Cordon Bleu cooking school.

He took the newspaper into the airport bar and ordered a glass of wine and a croquet monsieur sandwich, the classic French take on grilled ham and cheese. He leisurely ate it while looking through the newspaper.

Well, this is encouraging. I remember more than I thought I would. I know it's easier to read French than to speak it, but I think I'm going to be okay once English is no longer an option.

The photos and stories reassured him as he slowly began to immerse himself back into French culture. It had been a long time since he'd spent any time in France, but looking through the paper, it felt like yesterday. His sense of well-being was abruptly broken when his attention was drawn to a gruesome photograph of a young Afghan girl whose legs had been blown off by a roadside bomb. He put the rest of his sandwich down on the plate, having lost his appetite. He read every word of the article and looked at the picture again.

What are these animals thinking? What did that child ever do to deserve this? And what will happen to her? From what I've read, the Afghan men don't place a very high value on women anyway, and one without legs?

He could feel bile rising in the back of his throat. The wine was excellent, but Jordan couldn't finish it. All he could think about was the little girl, and what the future held for her. He wished he had someone he could talk to, thinking that at times like this the life he had chosen was downright lonely.

Numerous women had been more than happy to be wined and dined by him, but he'd always felt a wife and children would interfere with his traveling and his plan to eat at every

Michelin restaurant he could. Food, art, and wine had become his life.

In about thirty minutes he heard his flight being called and walked to the gate. It was a quick, uneventful flight, and Jordan was able to sleep for most of the hour and a half it took to fly to Marseille.

The captain's voice coming over the intercom woke him up. He retrieved his sling bag from the overhead bin, got his suitcase off of the conveyor belt, and walked out of the airport. He was about to get on the shuttle bus for the car rental agency when he saw a young man carrying a sign with his name on it. He approached the young man and said, *"Je suis Monsieur* Krame*r*."

"Monsieur Kramer, welcome to Marseille. I am Andre Lebeau. Chief Dubois asked me to pick you up and drive you to the chateau near the small village of St. Victor la Coste where you will be staying. He arranged for your rental car to be delivered to the chateau tomorrow morning. He thought you might enjoy a guide for your visit to Provence as the village is very small and hard to find. Even the taxi drivers have trouble finding it. I also have something in the trunk of my car that Chief Dubois said I should deliver to you."

"Monsieur," he continued, "I don't know the reason for your visit, but I am sure you will enjoy your stay in Provence. We are known for our wonderful food, wine and art."

Swell, Jordan thought, *at least at home I can run on the beach to work off the gourmet meals. It might be more of a challenge here. I don't want to get kicked off the police force for being overweight, and my parents' genes and my high metabolism can take me just so far. I better watch what I eat.*

He knew that probably wasn't going to happen, certainly not while he was in Provence.

Andre was a charming and intelligent companion. The three hour drive through the vineyards and olive groves from the airport to the chateau went quickly. Soon they were driving up a winding road. Even though it was dusk, Jordan could make out a low stone wall next to the road and the beautiful centuries' old chateaus scattered throughout the scenic countryside.

They turned into a cobblestone driveway leading to a large chateau situated on a knoll overlooking the valley below. Even from a distance, the chateau was incredibly beautiful. The walls around it were divided by two tall columns connected by a gate which served as an entrance. Behind the gate he could see a blue door, similar to so many he'd seen on the drive from Marseille.

A large covered porch stretched across the front of the chateau with white geraniums and blue lobelia spilling out of planters on either side of the blue door. He could just make out groves of trees which looked like orchards on the sides of the house with gravel pathways leading to them.

The entire scene was simply breathtaking. Jordan easily understood why this area had become such a popular tourist destination.

As the car passed through a gate and came to a stop in the large circular driveway, the door of the chateau opened and an imposing older woman walked out, accompanied by a younger man dressed in a traditional black and white hotel uniform.

"*Bonjour,* I am *Madame* Jolie Pascal. You must be *Monsieur* Kramer. We have been expecting you. Welcome to my home. Marc will show you to your room. Wine is served in the library at 7:00 p.m. and dinner is served at 8:00. If you need anything, please call the front desk."

Jordan thanked Andre for driving and told him he looked forward to seeing him again, perhaps at the end of his trip. Andre took a small case out of the trunk and handed it to Jordan. It contained the gun and police permit that Chief Lewis had requested from the Marseille Police Department. Jordan turned and followed Marc into the chateau.

They walked up the winding staircase, and although Jordan was an art connoisseur, he was also quite knowledgeable about antiques. He knew he was looking at some very valuable ones, and he couldn't believe the quality of the 18th and 19th century oil paintings displayed casually on the walls. Entering his room, he realized a great deal of money had been spent modernizing the chateau. Electricity, running water, a flat screen television, and a telephone had all been installed.

The French provincial furniture in his room looked like it had been in the chateau for many years. From his art history days he recognized the chair in the corner as being authentic, with its caned seat, cabriole legs, and simple scalloped carving which was repeated on the headboard and the dresser. A period lamp was on the nightstand and a marble bust was prominently displayed on the dresser. If the furniture hadn't been in the chateau for centuries, someone had taken a great deal of care decorating it to make sure that no period detail had been omitted.

His room overlooked a broad valley and rolling hills. Although it was almost dark, he could make out the chateau's vineyards and olive trees. He remembered being told that it was rude to ask how many acres of ranchland or farmland someone owned. Jordan assumed the same was true for vineyards, but he was sure that the Pascals' acreage had to be in the many hundreds. It was stunningly beautiful. The paintings of the Provence landscapes he had studied for years were reflected in the scene that unfolded before him.

He took a quick shower and washed away the travel grime. A few minutes later, he went downstairs. Hearing voices, he entered the library where wine was being served by *Madame* Pascal and a man Jordan assumed was her husband, *Monsieur* Pascal. He was as round and genial as his wife was ramrod thin and rigid.

What a strange couple, he thought. *Monsieur Pascal must be six inches shorter than she is and outweigh her by a hundred pounds. From the broken capillaries on his cheeks and nose, it looks like he thoroughly enjoys drinking the wines he produces in his vineyard.*

Monsieur Pascal walked over to Jordan and shook his hand while an ear-to-ear smile lit up his florid face. He had a large, droopy mustache beneath a mane of unruly white hair.

"Please," he said, "let me get you some wine. We're very proud of our wines and we're one of a growing number of organic vineyards. Would you prefer red or white? I think they're all good, but I've learned people usually have a preference."

The red and white wines of the Provence region were known throughout the world by wine connoisseurs. Jordan couldn't believe the array on the sideboard in front of him. Grenache, Syrah and Mourvédre reds and rosés along with Ugni Blanc and Rolle whites were all being freely poured. It was a French dream come true for Jordan.

"I prefer a red. What do you recommend?"

"You must try the Mourvédre. I'm told it's one of the best. Try a sip and tell me what you think."

Jordan swirled the wine in his glass and took a small sip. "Whoever told you that is absolutely right. It's wonderful. I'd like to try some of the others, but I think I've already found my favorite. Thank you."

"Bring your glass and I'll introduce you to the other guests."

Introductions were made, wine loosened tongues, and after some small talk, the group of ten made their way into the dining room.

Dinner was just as fabulous as the wines. Jordan loved French food, but so often chefs felt they couldn't leave well enough alone, adding their own touches and losing the essence of the dish. Not so at Chateau Pascal. Dinner was a simple cassoulet prepared in the classic tradition. It was peasant food at its best, enhanced by freshly baked bread and a salad that tasted as if it had been brought in directly from the garden.

Jordan was seated next to Madame Pascal. "I don't think I have ever tasted food that seemed this fresh. What's your secret?"

"What we don't grow on our own property, we get at local farmers' markets. They're held every day in the surrounding villages. We have chickens and also raise most of our own meat. I think you'll enjoy breakfast tomorrow morning. The fresh eggs, local bacon and fruit are usually a hit with our guests. Our cook comes in early to bake muffins and some other breakfast items. It's too dark now, but in the morning you will be able to see the orchards, our large vegetable gardens, and at this time of year, probably some quail. If you enjoy eating, you'll not do any better in France than here at Chateau Pascal."

Jordan could not have agreed more. "Thank you for an enjoyable evening. This has been a wonderful beginning for my stay in Provence."

He stood up and walked around the table, shaking hands with the other guests and the hosts. The dinner had been a nice respite from what he knew would be taking place in the next few days. He had paintings to locate and a thief to catch.

CHAPTER 7

After talking with Chief Lewis on the phone, Jordan's head was spinning as he got ready to go to dinner at Elena's. Seven paintings had been stolen from the Laguna Beach gallery. He'd seen one this afternoon. That left six. If Chief Lewis' suspicions were correct, that meant the other ones had possibly been bought by small galleries in villages located in the Provence area. He hoped to spend about six more days in the area, which meant he'd have to find one a day. The chances of him locating the right gallery where the other stolen paintings might be displayed were not particularly good. At a minimum, he figured he'd better plan on visiting at least three or four villages a day.

He took his laptop out of his luggage and began making notes of villages and galleries. Within an hour, he had a clear idea which villages had galleries. He mapped a route from St. Victor la Coste north to Lyon. There were over twenty galleries in the region, with the majority being in Avignon, Aix-en-Provence, Valence, Tain-l'Hermitage, Vienne and Lyon. He also located three in very small villages located off Route 7. Jordan decided to start his search for the stolen paintings in Lyon. He smiled to himself. He knew he'd find good food there.

Jordan subscribed to a number of food magazines. The night before he left Los Angeles he'd leafed through several looking for articles about good restaurants in Provence, particularly Michelin starred restaurants. Saveur magazine featured a long article about dining along Route 7, and listed several Michelin restaurants he was determined to try.

DIANNE HARMAN

Serendipity at its best. I can visit undiscovered art galleries and at the same time, get paid to eat some fantastic meals along the way. This really is the best of both worlds.

Jordan had put the two bottles of white wine he'd purchased in the large refrigerator in the chateau's kitchen before he'd called Chief Lewis. He walked downstairs and retrieved the bottles, putting them in the cloth sack the vintner had given him.

Elena's directions were easy to follow. Within minutes he could see the blue framed windows of her cottage in the light from the setting sun. As he turned onto the gravel drive leading to her cottage, he noticed large gardens on either side of the driveway. One looked like a nursery with beautiful brightly colored flowers fighting for attention. On the other side were rows of vegetables and herbs. Years ago several fruit trees had been planted along the stone fence which surrounded the property. He knocked on the blue painted door which was quickly opened by Elena.

"Welcome to my home. Please come in and make yourself comfortable," she said, holding the door open for him and motioning him into the kitchen.

Before he entered the cottage, he stood for a moment, looking at the plantings. "Your gardens are simply beautiful! You must spend a lot of time out here. By the way, I brought two bottles each of red wine and white wine," he said, following her into the kitchen and putting the sacks on the kitchen counter. "I didn't know what you'd be serving, and I wanted to make sure we had wine to match."

"I've fixed a beef daube which will go well with the red wine and the white wine will be perfect for the appetizer I've

39

made. Why don't you open the wine while I put the last touches on the appetizer and dinner? Let me get a wine opener for you."

Although the cottage was small, it was tastefully decorated. The Provence region was known for its blue and yellow fabrics. Elena had covered the couch and chairs with it and then reversed the colors in the fabric for the tablecloth and napkins. It was evident that Elena loved candles. Everywhere Jordan looked there was the play of candlelight against glass. A fire was crackling in the fireplace, and bouquets of fresh colorful flowers from the garden had been placed throughout the cottage. The outdoor riot of color was repeated inside.

Doors to two bedrooms and a bathroom led off the main room which consisted of a living room, kitchen and dining room. It was one of the most inviting homes Jordan had ever been in.

She placed a platter of baguettes on the coffee table. She'd lightly toasted them and spread a seasoned goat cheese on top with fresh tomato slices, basil, and lightly sautéed anchovies. The white wine Jordan had brought was the perfect accompaniment.

"Elena, this is wonderful. I assume the baguettes are from Henri's, but the tomatoes and basil must have come from your garden. You can taste the freshness. And the anchovies, they must be from Marseille. I've always heard that seafood from the Mediterranean is unequaled, and after the shrimp bisque at lunch and these anchovies, I'd have to agree."

"Yes, you can get very spoiled eating in this region. From what I've read, there are more Michelin rated restaurants here than anywhere else in the world. I've only visited a couple of them, but the food was incredible. You can tell from my garden that I love to eat and cook."

"What else do you do? I don't see signs of children, and you can only cook, work in the garden, and eat so much. I don't even see a television. What do you do with the rest of your time?"

"I'm a voracious reader. The Kindle was made for people like me. Any book I want is only one click away, and you can see that I don't have much extra space here for piles of books."

Even though her voice was animated, he noticed she was slumped against the back of the couch, running her hand back and forth against the fabric of her slacks. He'd questioned a lot of people during the twenty years he'd been with the LAPD, and she was exhibiting classic signs of someone who was lonely and depressed.

"What about friends and family? Do you have visitors from the States? Do you ever get lonesome? Do you think you'll stay here very long? You mentioned that you came here after your husband died. Have you thought about going back to California? I know that's too many questions all at once. I apologize, but I find your being here in Provence absolutely fascinating."

He didn't mention that he was used to interrogating people and even in social situations, he found he had a tendency to do it. He'd been told by a number of people he could be overbearing.

"I enjoy it here, particularly now that I'm working at Henri's. I think I'll probably be here for a long time. It's so beautiful and peaceful in Provence. I never want to go back to California," she replied.

Jordan didn't understand why, but he thought he noticed Elena's eyes beginning to tear up ever so slightly. He decided to change the subject. "Well, tell me, what do you like best about living here in the south of France?"

"I love the quiet and being able to do exactly what I want. I love the trust Henri has placed in me, allowing me to cook whatever's in season. He's a very generous man and I'm very lucky to be able to work for him. But enough about me, tell me more about yourself. Uh-oh, there goes the buzzer on the stove. Please, sit down at the table and pour us some red wine to go to with the beef. I'll bring the meal to the table."

She carried a heaping platter of beef daube over rich buttered noodles to the table. Carrots in a honey glaze and more fresh baguettes completed the meal. He couldn't believe his luck in being befriended by a woman who could cook like a Michelin chef and was breathtakingly beautiful as well.

"Elena, I need to tell you something. I wasn't completely candid with you earlier today. Actually, I'm a detective with the Art Theft Division of the Los Angeles Police Department." He stopped, noticing the slight involuntary flinch when he'd said he was a policeman. "Is anything wrong?"

"No, no. I took a large bite of the daube and it burned the roof of my mouth. I should know better. Please, go on. "

I knew it. I never should have asked him here. He doesn't seem suspicious of me, but maybe he's tailed me here and he's going to take me back to California. Dear God, a California detective!

"Well, this isn't for public knowledge, but I feel I can trust you. A couple from Laguna Beach who collect art recently spent some time in the Provence region, ate at Henri's, and then wandered around the village. They were surprised to see a California Impressionist artist by the name of Mitchell featured in the window of the art gallery in the village. A painting of the Marseille harbor, yes, a painting of the California Sierras, no. Then they remembered there'd been a theft of several paintings from a prominent Laguna Beach art gallery several months earlier, and wondered if there was a connection between the painting and the theft."

"I thought you said you worked for the Los Angeles Police Department. As I recall, Laguna Beach is quite a distance from Los Angeles."

She'd served the food family style at the table. He paused, "Elena, would you serve me some more daube and noodles? I know I shouldn't, but this is really delicious."

"I'm glad you like it. It's practically a staple here in France."

"Anyway, back to why I'm here. Yes, you're right. Laguna Beach is quite a ways from Los Angeles. I'm on loan to the Laguna Beach Police Department. The couple didn't have any way to find out if the painting they'd seen was the one that had been stolen. I happen to know them personally and I've advised them over the years about purchasing various paintings for their collection. They are very sophisticated art collectors and if their suspicions were aroused, I knew the painting was probably the Mitchell that had been stolen from the gallery."

He smiled warmly, trying to counteract the alarming image the word "police" often caused in people's minds. "I have to say this is definitely the best assignment I've ever had and meeting you has made it doubly so."

"Well, have you seen it? Is it the stolen painting?" she asked.

"Yes. I met with the owner of the gallery this afternoon, and I'm certain it's the stolen piece. In the next few days I'm going to visit other galleries in the area to see if any of the other paintings that were stolen were also brought to France to be sold. Care to accompany me? I can always use another set of eyes," Jordan asked, hoping against hope she'd say yes.

"I really wish I could, but I don't know anything about art. I would enjoy having someone teach me about what I'm looking at, but I'm already scheduled to work for the next three days. Henri has been so good to me, I can't let him down. However, I'll be off for two days after that. If those days work for you, I'd love to go gallery and restaurant hopping," Elena said, smiling.

DIANNE HARMAN

Good God, now I've done it. I could have gotten off without ever seeing him again, but instead I just suggested we spend time together on my days off. What am I thinking?

He stopped talking and just looked at her. She was stunningly beautiful and when she smiled, the world seemed to light up. Elena's figure was lush and filled with promise. Brown hair grazed her shoulders and her eyes were a mesmerizing shade of hazel. What Jordan didn't know was that brown dye covered Elena's natural jet black hair and green contacts over brown eyes created the unusual shade of hazel.

"Pick up your wine glass," she said, "and get comfortable in one of the upholstered chairs. We've been sitting on these hard chairs long enough." They spent the next two hours talking of this and that, simply getting to know each other. All too soon it was time for Jordan to leave.

"Don't forget your wine bottles," Elena said. "Let me get them for you."

"No, please keep them. Actually, if you'll have me, I'd like to come back tomorrow night for dinner. I love a good steak, and it's one of the few things I make well. I noticed you have a barbecue. Why don't I bring some steaks and potatoes? We can make a salad from whatever you have in your garden. I really want to see you again."

Before she could process his words, she found herself saying, "I'd love that. Drive safely and I'll see you tomorrow night about 7:00." She walked him to his car and before he got in, he leaned down and briefly kissed her on the cheek. "Thank you for dinner and a wonderful evening. I've really enjoyed being with you. See you tomorrow night."

45

Elena walked back in the house, for the first time acknowledging to herself that she was lonesome. She knew it was crazy to even think about it, but she wished she'd asked him to spend the night.

Oh yeah, that would really be smart. The best thing that could happen for me would be that he'd get hung up tomorrow and never come back here. How could I have met a police detective from California who came to Provence to investigate a crime, and I wind up inviting him to dinner? What was I thinking? And I just invited him for dinner again. I must either be crazy, or maybe I need to admit to myself that I really am lonesome. And I don't think I'm crazy.

She knew she was playing with fire, but it was as if there was an unseen magnetic force pulling her to Jordan. He was very attractive with his dark hair and a physique that showed it was exercised regularly. It had been a long time since she'd felt the warmth of a male body next to hers and she realized how much she missed it. Then she remembered he was a policeman and she felt a small shiver of fear run down her spine.

CHAPTER 8

Jordan got up early the next morning and decided to have breakfast when he got to Lyon. Although he'd found the Mitchell painting in a small village, he thought it would be prudent to begin his search for the other stolen paintings in a larger town. The thief might have started in Lyon and worked his way down to St. Victor la Coste, or perhaps he did it in reverse. It wasn't that far to Lyon, and Jordan wanted to be sure he wasn't missing anything. He planned on checking out a couple of galleries in Lyon, and then head to Vienne for a late lunch and more gallery hunting.

He awoke to a beautiful day, sunny skies, and just a nip of fall in the early morning air. The Renault started easily, and soon he was cruising north along Route 7. It was mid-September, the tourists were mostly gone, and the drive was beautiful. Although he'd read that July was the best time to see the fields of sunflowers and lavender in bloom, there were still hints of yellow and lavender carpeting the nearby hills.

Lyon was less picturesque than the countryside and was no exception to big-city traffic. Fortunately the parking structure he'd found was near the open-early, close-late restaurant he wanted to try.

He usually wasn't a fan of large restaurants, but the Belle Epoque setting of the Brasserie George Restaurant and the Michelin star were too tempting to pass up. He thought it must be good if it had survived for nearly two hundred years.

The maître d' led him to his table where a grey-haired waiter in a black bolero jacket and bow tie delicately opened a snow-white napkin and placed it in his lap.

"*Monsieur*, here is some bottled water for you. May I get you something else to drink while you look at the menu, maybe some fresh-squeezed orange juice?"

"*Oui*, though I am in a bit of a hurry. Orange juice, some coffee and two pains au chocolate. *Merci beaucoup*."

He eagerly anticipated the chocolate croissants, a deviation from his usual healthy breakfast. In spite of a deep love of food, and studying at the Cordon Bleu, Jordan had never mastered the art of gourmet cooking. He'd tried, but between working long hours, and being extremely impatient, he'd decided long ago that croissants and everything else tasted much better prepared by someone else.

While he was eating the best croissants he'd ever had, he looked at the map of Lyon he'd stuck in his pocket before he left the chateau. The three galleries he wanted to visit weren't that far apart, and were actually quite close to the restaurant. He paid his bill, tipping generously, and headed back to work.

Jordan walked down the street looking at the shopkeepers as they gaily greeted one another. They watered the profusion of bright flowers in containers outside their doors and swept the entryways to their shops as they prepared to open them. He spotted a red awning with the words in white, "Galerie Bernard" and right below them, "Beaux-Arts."

The gallery was much larger than the gallery in St. Victor la Coste. White walls highlighted the paintings of the

Provence area with landscape scenes depicting fields of lavender, sunflowers, vineyards and olive groves. The vibrant colors of the countryside were captured by the paintings in gilt brushed frames, but there were no works by any California artists on display.

When he was back on the sidewalk, he took the city map out of his pocket, looked at it, and walked the short distance to the second gallery, Galerie Denis, with white lettering on its colorful blue awning indicating its name.

Although it wasn't as large as Galerie Bernard, it, too, was roomier than the one he'd been in yesterday. The softly toned flesh colored walls were a perfect backdrop to a huge variety of paintings, ranging from chateaus to pheasants to bottles of wine. Again, there was no artwork by a California Impressionist.

Two doors away, he spotted the green and white awning of the last of the galleries. It was much smaller than the other two and there, prominently displayed in the window, was a painting by Edgar Payne. He stopped for a moment, his heart pounding.

My God, the chief's hypothesis was right. The thief may have brought all of the paintings to the Provence area and sold them to small galleries where they'd be much less likely to be identified as stolen.

He walked into the Galerie Lebeau and was greeted by a beautiful young woman. *"Bon jour Monsieur*, my name is Colette. How may I help you?"

When he was a student at the Cordon Bleu, Jordan had found French women to be utterly charming. Colette was no exception. Short black hair in a pixie cut, leggings with a long tunic, and a casual scarf thrown around her shoulders added to the chicness that French women always seemed to possess. Jordan wondered how they managed to pull off their casual sense of elegance so nonchalantly.

"I was just walking by and I'm curious about the painting you have in the window, the one by the California artist. I'm homesick for California. How much is it and how did it happen to come here? May I take a closer look at it?"

"You are welcome to look at it. As to your other questions, *Monsieur,* I don't know the answers. My father owns the gallery. When I came home on a school break from university, it was here. Let me call him for you."

"I would appreciate it. Thank you."

He watched her dial the number. She began to speak very rapidly in French, faster than he could follow. While she was talking, he examined the painting.

The frame was similar to the one he'd seen on the Mitchell at Galerie Reynaud. The frames on both were much newer than the paintings and were clearly not the originals. They were more ornate, more of a European style than American. Colette listened on the phone for what seemed like a long time, hung up and turned to Jordan.

"*Monsieur*, my father said that a man brought it in a few months ago. It is a bit different from what we usually carry, but my father looked it up and realized it was by a well-known

California artist. He hoped to sell it to an American tourist, but the season is almost over and he has had no buyers. He wanted 17,000 euros, but he told me he would now take 15,000.

"He remembered the man who sold it to him because he asked if my father could recommend a good authentic Lyon restaurant. He had been to Brasserie George for lunch and wanted to eat dinner in a restaurant of that caliber. Does that help you?"

"You've been very helpful. Thank you. Let me think about it. Do you have a card?"

"*Oui*. If we can help, please call us. The painting really is spectacular. I think it's better than most California art I have studied. I understand that the artist is very well known in the United States and that his work is highly regarded, as well as being very desirable."

Jordan's mind was spinning as he left the gallery. He was certain he was going to find the other paintings, but then what? He didn't know how he was going to determine the identity of the thief. So far all he knew was that stolen paintings from a Laguna Beach gallery had made their way to two small galleries in Provence, and that they had been sold to the galleries by a man who liked to dine in fine restaurants. That wasn't much to go on. Jordan walked to the parking structure where he had left his car and slowly drove from there to Route 7.

CHAPTER 9

Jordan spent the short time on the drive to Vienne fantasizing about Elena. There was a sense of mystery about her that only added to her allure. He could easily visualize Elena in the nude. He could feel her soft skin as he caressed her. Jordan wanted her. And when it came to women, Jordan usually got what he wanted.

The small village of Vienne was located on the west bank of the Rhone River. He parked the car near the Restaurant de la Pyramide which was located in a hotel. He understood why architects considered this small town to be nirvana. The Roman influence was still evident in the temple ruins, churches and an incredible statue of Saint Peter. The remains of the majestic Gothic cathedral of St. Maurice rose from a terrace overhanging the river. The sense of history in the village was almost palpable and he found himself enchanted.

Jordan walked into the hotel where the restaurant was located and soon was seated at a table loaded with fresh flowers and a gleaming white tablecloth. Everywhere he looked, bouquets of flowers, looking and smelling freshly picked, filled the room. He glanced at the menu and decided to order the market lunch. It was a simple but elegant meal, consisting of a cheese platter with three cheeses: a buttery brie, a bold Etorki, and a classic blue Roquefort. Freshly baked bread, crunchy nuts, sweet pears, and cantaloupe were served with the cheese plate. The food was everything he'd come to expect in Provence.

He looked at his watch - time to get back to work. The art gallery he wanted to see in Vienne was only a short walk away. The narrow cobblestoned streets were smooth and worn after centuries of use by people, carts, and horses. Floral containers hung from every window with brightly colored geraniums in lavender, red, and white spilling out of them. The gallery was located in the middle of the block and Jordan could see that the door was open. As he got closer to the gallery, he saw a Granville Redmond painting prominently displayed in the window. *Bingo. I've nailed three of them.*

Jordan walked through the open door and was immediately greeted by the young man behind the desk. *"Bon jour, Monsieur*, I am Gabriel, how may I help you?" he asked.

"I'm an art dealer from California, and I have a client who collects Granville Redmond paintings. May I see the one in the window?"

"Oui," he said, taking the painting from the easel which had been supporting it. "It's quite colorful. I have not been to the United States, but the man who sold the painting to the gallery owner said this painting showed the hills of Laguna Beach in spring."

Jordan had been to Laguna Beach many times and the young man was right. The painting clearly reflected springtime, when the hills above the city are carpeted in blue and orange flowers.

"Can you tell me something about the person who sold it to the gallery?" Jordan asked. "I'm curious as to why someone would sell a piece of this type of art to a French gallery rather than put it up for auction where Californians would be more apt to see it and buy it."

53

"I don't know much about him, but he was very interesting-looking. There was something ..." Gabriel seemed to be embarrassed.

"Yes?" prompted Jordan.

"Well...I am an art student. Drawing is my area of interest. I wanted to take a picture of him to use for a study later. Not surprisingly, he said absolutely no when I asked him, but I took one anyway using the gallery's old Polaroid camera when he wasn't looking."

Gabriel looked guilty. "Please don't tell anyone. I took it when the owner went to the back room to get his checkbook to pay for the painting. He would not be happy with me if he knew about it."

"May I see it?"

"Of course," he said, reaching into a far corner in the back of the desk drawer. "Here, this is the photograph of the man who sold the painting to the gallery."

"Thank you. Is there anything else you remember about him?"

"He is French and I believe he said he has family in the area. He talked a lot about food and asked me to tell him which restaurants in the area were really good. He was quite portly. I remember thinking he looked like a chef. In fact, he had a number of scars on his arms along with a tattoo of a French chef's knife. My uncle is a chef and has a similar tattoo on his arm. Many French chefs have it tattooed on their arms."

54

The back doorbell rang and Gabriel excused himself, disappearing through the curtain that hid the back door. Jordan immediately got out his cell phone and took several close-up shots of the Polaroid photo. He could hardly believe his luck.

He put his phone away and examined the painting. He noticed that the same type of frame that had been used on the other two paintings had been used on this painting as well. The seller must have smuggled the stolen paintings into France unframed, which made sense. They wouldn't take up as much space and would be easier to smuggle.

A thief and also a fellow gourmand. Well, isn't that interesting. I wonder if it would be worthwhile to show his picture to employees at high-end restaurants in the area. Maybe they can tell me something. I wonder if he could have eaten at Henri's Bakery when he was in St. Victor la Coste.

He made a mental note to show the photos he'd taken to Elena that night at dinner. If the seller was as interested in food as he seemed to be, he probably would have eaten at Henri's, and Elena might remember him.

"What is the price of the Redmond piece?" he asked Gabriel when he returned. "I will need to take that into consideration when I advise my client."

"*Certainement, Monsieur.* Let me look at the ledger." He took a large leather book out of the bottom drawer of the old roll-top desk. Jordan was amused at the quaintness of the gesture, thinking of the highly computerized galleries in California. "I see that the owner of the gallery would like to have 152,000 euros, but I think he would take less. I would be happy to ask him. I could call you tomorrow."

"Yes, thank you. I would like to know so I can discuss it with my client. I'm sure you don't mind if I take a few pictures of the painting for him. I was just walking down the sidewalk when I saw it. You've been very helpful. Let me give you my business card."

Many years ago Jordan had business cards printed with the phony name of a gallery, no address and his cell phone number on it. He took one from his wallet and gave it to Gabriel. "Again, thank you. I'll look forward to your call." He walked out the door and down the cobblestone street to where his car was parked.

On his drive back to Chateau Pascal he made a mental list of what he needed to do. As soon as he returned to his room, he needed to email the chief and tell him about Gabriel's thoughts on the seller being a chef and French.

The photo was a superb piece of luck. He could send it to the chief and have him search through the database of passport photographs maintained by the U.S. Immigration authorities to see if there were any possible matches. Jordan couldn't access the high-security system himself in Provence, but the chief could.

If they could find out the name of the man in the photograph, Jordan might be able to locate the seller's family and get more information about the suspected thief.

He parked his car at the far end of the driveway and walked up the curved staircase to his room, pausing for a few moments to look at the art on the walls.

There must be a fortune in art, just on the walls of the staircase. I wonder if this is even the good stuff, or if they have that in their private area of the chalet?

When he got to his room he wasted no time, emailing Chief Lewis a brief report of what he had seen and discovered, concluding with the photographs he had taken. He attached the photos and report to an email, and sent them to the chief, feeling a sense of relief.

Good job. Now I'm off to dinner with a woman I would like to get to know in several ways. Ahh - great art, wine, food, and a deliciously tantalizing woman. This is definitely not a bad gig!

CHAPTER 10

On one of the rare occasions Elena opened the closet in the second bedroom of the cottage, the one she'd made into a den, the first thing she spotted was a laptop computer in its case. She'd opened the closet, looking for a fresh tablecloth for dinner that evening with Jordan.

She and Jeffrey had used the laptop to keep track of the motel finances. She'd grabbed it and brought it with her to Provence when she hurriedly left the Blue Coyote Motel after Jeffrey's death. When she rented the cottage in Provence, she'd put it against the back wall of the closet and forgotten about it.

I wish I'd never brought the damn thing with me. It just reminds me of the hours Jeffrey spent in front of it, doing whatever it was he was doing. I thought I might need it, but so far I haven't. Maybe I should just get rid of it. There's a little computer store in the village. I wonder if they'd want to buy it. I probably better make sure that Jeffrey wasn't looking at child porn on it when he used it. I know in California if a technician finds child porn on a computer, he has to report it. Maybe there's a law like that here in France, and I don't want to spend time in a French jail.

She took it out of the closet, put it on the desk and plugged it in. It had been several months since she'd used it and it took a while to get it up and running. In a few minutes she saw the familiar grey apple on the screen as it booted up. She sat down at the small desk in the den, trying to remember what password she'd used to gain access. Finally it came to her and she typed in "MARJEF." She remembered Jeffrey once saying that even though he was the one who would use it most of the time, she'd need an easy to remember password and what could be easier than a combination of their names, Maria and Jeffrey. She smiled, thinking about the man Jeffrey was before he went mad. It was just like him to want to make life easy for her. Just as he had with the two drugs he'd provided for her, the anti-aging hormone and Freedom, the "feel-good" drug.

I wonder if I'm starting to show my age. I see myself in the mirror every day, so I don't know if there's a big difference from what I looked like before and what I look like now. I'd give anything to take the pills Jeffrey formulated for the motel guests – the combination of anti-aging and Freedom. I'd have the best of both worlds, feeling good all the time and I wouldn't age. He really was a genius.

This is weird. I haven't used this thing for months. I think the last time I used it was to do the bookkeeping for the motel about a month before I left and I probably researched some recipes. Well, I don't need the bookkeeping program anymore, so I'll just delete it.

She looked at the screen as the familiar icons appeared on the desktop home page. There were very few. Jeffrey used it to search out certain plants and things he wanted to use in his experiments. Other than that the standard icons that came with the laptop were the only things showing on the screen. Suddenly her attention was caught by a file she'd never seen before. It was simply labeled "Jeffrey."

That's odd. I sure don't remember that being there. I wonder if he added something I don't know about. She clicked on the file. There were three items in it. Her heart began to speed up and she could feel herself perspiring. She couldn't believe what she was seeing. The first sheet was labeled "Hormone," the second sheet "Freedom," and the third sheet, "Guest Pill."

She clicked on the "Hormone" sheet. There were six rows with numbers along with what looked like plant names. "Freedom" had eight rows of numbers and plant names. "Guest Pill" had fourteen rows of numbers and plant names.

Oh my God. Am I imagining this? Could Jeffrey have been worried he was losing his mind and put his secret formulas on the laptop? Could these pages be his formulas?

She got up and went to the kitchen for a glass of water. Her hands were shaking so badly she had to put both of them around the glass to get it to her lips. She went back to the computer and sat down. Elena pinched herself to see if this was a dream. She wondered if you wanted something badly enough, if your mind could play tricks and tell you that you'd found it. She looked again. The three formulas were right in front of her on the screen.

I don't have a printer so I better make a note of these before the computer breaks down and I lose them.

She opened the desk drawer and pulled out a notepad. She began to carefully transcribe all three of the formulas, checking and double checking to make sure what she had written down was an exact replica of what was shown on the computer. Elena turned the laptop off, grabbed her iPad and went out on the patio. She opened it up and began researching the names of the plants Jeffrey had listed in the formulas. All of them were from South America and after an hour of research, she determined that only drug companies could bring them into the United States from Mexico, where they were distilled. The drug companies were a powerful lobby and they'd been able to get a Trade Agreement in place because the plants were essential in many of the drugs that they formulated.

Elena began pacing the length of the patio. All she could think about was getting the drug. What she really needed was a chemist. Even though she had the names of the plants and the amounts, there had to be more to it than that. At the bottom of each of the pages were notations which she'd painstakingly copied, but they didn't mean a thing to her. Maybe they would to a chemist, but how was she supposed to find a chemist in this little village? Plus, Jeffrey was one of the finest chemists in the world. It might take a very knowledgeable chemist to understand his notations.

I need to let this settle in. There's nothing I can do today, but maybe, just maybe, I can get the drug again. Now I need to get ready for Jordan. I don't have much time and there's no way I can tell him about the formulas without going into everything that happened on my last afternoon at the Blue Coyote Motel.

CHAPTER 11

Jordan left the chateau and walked to the parking lot, got in his car and drove the short distance to the *épicier*. While the butcher cut T-bone steaks from the loin of beef hanging in the back cooler, Jordan selected two large potatoes and a few other items. He couldn't pass up the Chateuneuf-du-Pape Cotes du Rhône wine and bought two bottles.

He made his way up the winding hill, spotted the blue shutters, and saw that candles had already been lit in the house. The winding path to the door had several lighted pillar candles in tall glass hurricane holders as well. It made the appearance of the cottage seem even more warm and inviting than it had been the evening before, almost magical.

I must have passed some test. This looks promising.

Elena opened the door just as he raised his hand to knock. "Let me help you with those sacks. What did you bring? This looks like more than steak and potatoes," she said.

She wore jeans and a simple pink and white striped blouse. She'd cut her long hair right after she landed in Marseilles, but it had grown quite a bit since then. Elena wore it pulled behind her ears, with bangs swept to the side. On her ears were big hoop earrings and gold bracelets jangled on her wrists. She looked fresh and beautiful. Jordan beamed at her.

"I couldn't resist," he answered. "I'm a sucker for Chateuneuf-du-Pape wine, and it wouldn't be a true baked potato without bacon and sour cream. I thought you'd probably have

62

some chives or scallions in your garden. Why don't you put the potatoes in the oven and I'll open the wine?"

While he was opening the wine, he stole a glance at Elena. She really was beautiful. He couldn't even begin to guess her age. There were no lines on her face or around her eyes. With all of the investigations Jordan had conducted over the years, he'd become pretty good at gauging a person's age, but not in Elena's case. None of the usual benchmarks were there.

He couldn't remember if Elena had worn make-up the day before, but she certainly had applied some tonight and applied it well. Her hazel eyes were glowing with her long lashes darkened by mascara and soft brown eyeliner applied to the lids. Her cheeks were a little more blushed than he remembered and she wore a hint of lipstick. He wondered what it would be like to kiss those soft, inviting lips. He didn't know how long she'd been widowed or how long it had been since she'd been with a man. When they met yesterday and during dinner last night, he'd sensed some sexual tension between them, but tonight was a different story. Sex was definitely in the air, like a thick perfume.

Elena washed the potatoes, pierced and oiled them, and put them in the oven. She felt fabulous, the best she'd felt in a long time. After she finished working at Henri's Bakery earlier in the day, she'd headed to the village pharmacy with its vast array of make-up and skin products.

As she was getting ready for the evening, and applying make-up for the first time in months, she realized how much she'd missed being attractive. If that was vanity, so be it. Her mother's mantra came back to haunt her: *Get a good job. Find a rich man. Get out of the barrio.*

COYOTE IN PROVENCE

Well, Madre, I did that and look what happened. I got out of the barrio and ended up in Provence with no man, just a dead husband. Maybe her mantra was wrong for me. And now look what I've done – invited a policeman for dinner for the second night in a row. Maybe I like to live on the edge a little more than I thought. This could really be dangerous for me, but somehow, I just don't care. Anyway, I'm lonely and he's very attractive.

Elena took the glass of wine that Jordan offered her. "We have some time before the potatoes will be ready. Let's go out on the patio. It's such a beautiful evening," she said.

Large wooden baskets of flowering plants hung from the patio's open lattice cover. Numerous clay pots filled with a variety of brightly colored flowers had been carefully arranged on the tiled floor. There was a charming small table and chairs, with soft pillows cutting the harshness of the wrought iron. In the distance, the lights of the village sparkled in the last glow of daylight. The hills were bathed in muted shades of purples and blues. They raised a glass to one another in a silent toast.

"Tell me about your day," she began as she took a sip of her wine. "Did you find any of the paintings you were looking for?"

"As a matter of fact," he said, "It has been a very successful day. I located two more paintings, and I was able to get a photo of the person who sold a painting to one of the galleries. I ate in two fabulous restaurants, and the day isn't over yet!"

She laughed. "You're setting a pretty high bar for me. I'm not a professional chef from a fancy restaurant. I just like to cook."

"Elena, don't downplay your cooking. And I guarantee you that the chefs in the restaurants did not look like you. You look absolutely stunning tonight. And I'd be a liar if I didn't tell you how much I've looked forward to seeing you again."

Their eyes met and they were both silent for a moment. "I feel the same way, Jordan. I know you're only going to be here for a few days, but I'm glad you came to Henri's and asked to speak with me. I've been looking forward to this all day as well. I didn't realize how lonely I've been."

"I'm glad to hear that."

Elena jumped ahead, not waiting for the questions she knew he'd be asking at some point. "My husband was very ill before he died. It's been a long time since I have enjoyed being with a man, and even more, had the feeling a man was enjoying being with me. Thank you for that."

They began to speak at the same time and then laughed, breaking the tension of the moment. "Elena, I'll only be here for a few days. I'd like to make them memorable for both of us." Jordan stood up, setting his wine glass on the table. "I may be really misreading things, but I want you, and I think you feel the same way. If we were back in the United States, we could do a long mating dance, but we don't have the luxury of time."

He leaned over and gave her a long, passionate kiss which she eagerly returned. "Please, beautiful lady that I hardly know, won't you come with me?" He extended his hand to her. She took it and stood, putting her wine glass on the table as well.

They walked into the house and into her bedroom. She started to unbutton her blouse. "Stop," Jordan said. "I want to take off your clothes, one by one." He finished unbuttoning her blouse and deftly undid the front clasp of her bra, freeing her full, heavy breasts. "My God, you're even more beautiful than I thought."

He began to gently caress her nipples with one hand while he put his other hand behind her head, pulling her mouth to his. He kissed her passionately. She could feel his hard-on pushing against his jeans. "Jesus, Elena. I don't know how long I can last."

He unzipped her jeans while she unbuttoned his shirt and undid his jeans, releasing his fully erect penis as he stepped out of them. Elena's clothes dropped off, revealing silk and lace underwear. The blue thong covered her lush pubic area, and she could feel herself becoming wet with desire.

Jordan sat down on the bed and pulled her to him, kissing her breasts. He pulled the thong down and she stepped out of it. She straddled him, gently guiding his pulsating erection into her wetness. She began to move up and down in a slow erotic manner. Jordan couldn't take it any longer. "Elena, get off of me and lie down. Hurry, I want to feel every part of you!"

Afterward, when Jordan was capable of speaking, he said, "I'm crushing you." He rolled off and pulled her to him. They stayed that way for a long time, each lost in their own thoughts.

I've never felt this sexually attracted to any woman. What in the hell is going on? I don't really know anything about her. Talk about an affair to remember. This is the one. And me,

66

the one the rest of the detectives call "Mr. Cautious," because I'm so careful about the women I see. This is completely unlike me, but there's something irresistible about her.

My God, Elena thought. *What have I done? I've never had a sexual experience like what just happened. I don't want it to end. But a detective, and one from Southern California? Thank God he's leaving soon. I'm just going to enjoy the next few days and then he'll be on his way and my world will be back to normal. I'll never see him again, and that's probably for the best.*

"Up, beautiful lady. I'm starving. I'll get dressed and light the barbecue. See you outside."

They dined on baked potatoes, steak, salad and fresh bread. The chocolate mousse Elena had made earlier for dessert stayed in the refrigerator as they eagerly returned to her bedroom after dinner.

"Jordan, please spend the night."

"You have no idea how much I want to," he said as he kissed her, "but I need to get back to the chateau and see if Chief Lewis has sent me anything. You do remember that this is a business trip?"

"What kind of business?" she whispered as she gently unzipped his pants and slipped her hand inside the opening.

Much later he left her and drove to the chateau. After he left, she stood in front of the mirror, searching for wrinkles.

COYOTE IN PROVENCE

Could it be? Could I have found the formulas that keep people from aging and feeling depressed? I wouldn't have to age and I'd never have to be depressed again. But now what? I'll need a chemist and the ingredients. I'll think about it tomorrow, when I'm not so tired.

CHAPTER 12

Jordan rolled over and looked at the bedside clock. It was 8:00 a.m., which was extremely late for him. *Well, I can justify this one. I didn't get back to my room until well after 2:00 a.m.*

He smiled as he thought back to the previous night. *That is one hell of a woman. I can't remember ever spending a night like that.* They'd made love before dinner and twice after dinner.

Jordan walked over to the desk and retrieved his cell phone. Chief Lewis had emailed him a memo.

Thanks for the photographs and doing such a good job. I'm shopping the man's photo around, trying to find someone who can identify him. I've contacted a friend of mine who works for U.S. Immigration and Customs Enforcement. I'm hoping he can get the photo put into their new machine which matches submitted photos with passport photos. I want you to continue what you're doing and get back to me when you have more information to report.

It was 9:00 a.m. by the time he showered and dressed. He was having dinner at Elena's house that night, but he planned on spending the day in the Tain-l'Hermitage and Valence area.

He decided to dress like a businessman who was visiting galleries between appointments. He put on a lightweight blue pin-striped suit, a white shirt and a muted striped tie. He added glasses and a false mustache. Jordan looked in the mirror, satisfied with his reflection. Although he didn't think he'd aroused suspicion yesterday, he wanted to play it safe with the disguise. At the last minute he put a photo of the purported chef and possible thief, in his sling bag, planning to show it to chefs working in nearby restaurants in hopes they might recognize the man in the photo.

The drive was charming. Rolling hills with old stone cottages dotted the landscape. Large chateaus were on top of many of the hills, with sprawling vineyards and olive groves leading up to them. Along the road weathered men in berets prodded animals with sticks that had been sharpened with knives. It was a step back in time.

Two hours later he walked into Le Routier 7, a beige building which had a bright blue door and blue window coverings. The parking lot was full of trucks. It looked like the articles he'd read about the restaurant had been right - it seemed to be a trucker's paradise. Jordan ordered scrambled eggs and a croissant as the attentive waiter filled his coffee cup. He took the photo from his sling bag.

"*Monsieur*," Jordan said to the waiter, "do you know who the man is in this photograph? I believe he is a chef."

"*Non*, but I have not been working here very long. Let me send our chef out. He might know him." Several minutes later a tall, thin, grey-haired man with an apron tied at his waist appeared next to his table.

"David tells me that you have a question regarding a man in a photograph. How may I help you?" the gracious chef asked.

"*Monsieur,* do you recognize this man? I understand he is a chef, and I would like to talk to him about a restaurant some clients of mine are opening in California. Do you know anything about him?"

The chef took the photo and walked over to the window where the light was streaming in. He looked at it for several minutes and returned to Jordan's table. "I am not sure, but it looks very much like Pierre Yount. We met through mutual friends when he studied at the Cordon Bleu, but I have not seen him for many years. I believe his family is from the Avignon area. That's all I know. I hope it helps," he said.

You have no idea. "Merci beaucoup. Yes, it definitely helps. Thank you for your time and the information."

He finished his breakfast, anxious to visit the galleries. The village was quite small. There was one large street with several outdoor cafes. At the far end of the street was the daily farmer's market. Lanes led off the main street, and he could see old houses and stone cottages separated by trees that looked as if they'd been there for centuries.

Jordan was surprised that a village this small could support two galleries. Both of them primarily featured the artwork of the owners, but at the second one, hanging on the back wall, was a painting by another California Impressionist artist, Guy Rose. It was a magnificent piece depicting the cliffs of Laguna Beach in various shades of tans set against the deep blue of the ocean. The shallow water at the base of the cliffs was green where the waves lapped against the smooth rocks.

"*Monsieur,*" a distinguished looking man said as he hurried over to Jordan, "I am Blaise Thiers, the owner of the gallery. I'm sorry for not greeting you when you walked in, but I wanted to finish up with *Madame* Lesalle. Thank you for being so patient."

"That's fine. I was just admiring this painting. Can you tell me something about it?"

"Yes. It's by Guy Rose, a California artist. The galleries in this area specialize in landscape paintings, and although this is not one of our traditional landscapes, I thought the cliffs and the ocean were beautiful. I bought it several months ago. You see, many Parisian galleries send representatives to this area to buy art. I borrowed heavily to buy the painting and hoped that one of them would be interested. I thought I could make a large profit from it. Now I wonder if that was wise."

"How much are you asking for it?"

"In US dollars it would be about $175,000. I know that sounds like a lot of money, but when I researched it I found very few of his paintings on the market. I decided on that price because it is low for a high quality Rose painting such as this one."

"I'd like to ask you something." Jordan took the photograph of Pierre Yount out of his sling bag. "*Monsieur* Thiers, is this the man who sold you the painting?"

"Yes, that is him. I don't know his name. He asked that the painting's price be paid to an account in Avignon. He said his family was selling some of their art because his father was in poor health."

DIANNE HARMAN

"Did you notice if he had a tattoo on his arm?" Jordan asked.

"Yes. It was a chef's knife. I was rather surprised that a man of his age would have such a tattoo. Younger men have them, but not men in their late 40's or early 50's."

Bingo. I don't even have to ask him the age of the chef. I'm having another very good day.

"Thank you. You've been very helpful. May I take your business card and would you mind if I took a photograph of the painting? I have a client who collects California Impressionists and he may be interested."

"Yes, here's my card and please, take a photo of it and show it to your client. Several galleries in Paris have expressed interest, but so far none of them has made an offer."

"Again, thank you for your help," Jordan said after he had taken several photos of the painting. He left the gallery and walked two blocks to where his car was parked.

He drove the short distance to Valence, located three of the galleries he'd mapped out, and found his way to Pic le 7, a rare 3-star Michelin restaurant. He wasn't disappointed. He'd eaten a light breakfast in anticipation of the meal, which was heavenly.

Jordan feasted on pan bagnat, a type of open-faced sandwich. It was beautifully arranged with tomatoes, green beans, tuna, and sliced hard-boiled eggs tossed in a light vinaigrette dressing served on a toasted split sourdough roll, and covered with lightly fried anchovies. It was a feast for the eyes

73

and the mouth. A glass of rosé wine and a tapenade made with olives from nearby groves completed the meal.

Even though he was certain he couldn't eat any more, he succumbed to the waiter's dessert suggestion of a specialty of the region, gateau labully, an orange blossom scented brioche with pink pralines.

He took the photograph of *Monsieur* Yount out of his sling bag. "*Monsieur*," he asked the waiter, do you know this man? He is a chef."

"*Non*, but if I may borrow the photograph, I will show it to Chef Binet."

"*Certainement*."

A few minutes later he returned. "*Monsieur*, Chef Binet says that the man in the photograph is *Monsieur* Yount, a chef he studied with at the Cordon Bleu. He says that he hasn't seen him in years and has no idea where he is now. He hopes that helps."

"*Merci beaucoup*. You've been most helpful. Please tell the chef I thank him very much for his information."

It was just after 2:00 p.m., the time the galleries re-opened from their lunch break. He got in his car and parked a few blocks from the next gallery he wanted to visit. He sat there for a few moments letting his lunch settle as he thought over what he'd found out about the mysterious Pierre Yount.

I know he's a chef. I know he's sold stolen art to galleries in Provence. I still don't know why. I don't know if he stole the paintings, or if someone else did and he's just fencing

74

them for the thief. I know he has a tattoo of a knife on his arm. I know what he looks like and people have told me his parents live in the area. I'm lucky I've found out that much, but it's still not a lot to go on.

He got out of his car and leisurely walked to the gallery. When he entered a bell tinkled, but no one came out to greet him. He stood for a moment, letting his eyes adjust to the muted light in the gallery. He looked around, and there in the middle of several Provence landscape scenes, was a Donna Schuster hillside landscape watercolor.

Good grief. I remember from my art history days that she was really well-known for her watercolors. I think she even earned a silver medal for one that was shown at the Los Angeles Museum of History, Science and Arts sometime around 1914. This is getting more and more interesting. All of the stolen paintings are landscape scenes which in some way fit in well with the Provence region. All of them have been reframed in similar frames. All of them have asking prices far less than what they would command at either California galleries or auction houses.

"*Monsieur*, may I trouble you for a moment?" Jordan asked the harried shopkeeper as he came into the gallery from the back room.

"*Oui*, what do you want?"

"I have two questions. Could you tell me what you are asking for the Schuster painting? And is the man in this photograph the man you bought the Schuster from?"

"The price is $2,500 in US dollars. That's far less than what the painting is worth. Why do you want to know about the seller? I own the painting, and no, that is not the man I bought it from," he said belligerently.

"Are you sure that the man in the photograph is not the man you bought the painting from?"

"I told you it's not, didn't I? I can't help you. Excuse me. I have things I need to do," he said, turning away from Jordan.

"Thank you. If the man who sold you the painting should return, would you call me? Here is my card."

He left, knowing that the owner was very suspicious of him and would never call, even if the seller returned.

It looks like Pierre must have an accomplice, at least when it comes to selling the paintings. Maybe the other man stole the paintings and Pierre is selling them because he's French. So now I'm looking for two men. I thought it was a little too cut and dried. I don't know who stole the paintings, and I have no motive other than that someone is getting money from the gallery owners for these stolen paintings.

And why would the thief steal paintings valued from $250,000 to $2,500? That doesn't make sense. The only thing I can think of is that he took what was easiest to grab off of the wall of the gallery and quickly get out of the gallery. I need to have the chief find out if the stolen paintings were displayed on the same wall, or if they were physically close to one another.

The next two galleries yielded no stolen paintings. By now it was 3:00 p.m. and Jordan was tired. He had a two hour drive ahead of him. He wasn't going to Elena's cottage until 7:00 that evening and he could use a nap, even if it was short. If last night was any indication, he needed to regain some of his strength.

When he returned to the chateau he stretched out on the bed, and immediately fell asleep. Fortunately, he'd set the alarm clock because it took him quite awhile to come out of his deep sleep and turn it off. He laid there for several minutes, trying to recreate the dream he'd had of a woman who looked a lot like Elena. All he could remember was that she was dressed in a ghost-like gauzy gown and shrouded in mist. He'd tried to touch her, but whenever he got close enough, she disappeared, only to return a few feet away. He smiled, remembering the very warm Elena of last night who had eagerly responded to his touch.

Jordan took a quick shower and left for her cottage.

CHAPTER 13

It had been a long day for Elena. She hadn't had much sleep the night before and to make matters worse, the restaurant had been busier than usual for a mid-week day. Henri was constantly being told how wonderful his new luncheon chef was, and he knew he'd been very lucky to hire her before someone else did.

"Elena, you look tired, and you've been working very hard these last few weeks. Why don't you take an extra day off tomorrow? We can do without you for a couple of days, and when you come back, you'll feel rejuvenated. And I hear there might be a very good reason that you're so tired, in addition to working in the restaurant." Henri's eyes sparkled with laughter.

Good grief, are there no secrets in this village? I'll bet everyone knows exactly when Jordan came to my cottage last night and when he left and they could probably figure out what went on in between. So much for trying to develop female relationships here. Now the village women will be certain that I'm after their husbands.

"Ahh, Henri, I don't know what you mean, but I could use an extra day off. Thank you so much. I'll see you in three days. *Bon jour.*"

Two hours later, she heard the Renault coming up the lane and ran out to greet Jordan. He got out of the car, put his arms around her and kissed her deeply. "Elena, I missed you today. I can't believe it, but I did. I wish you could be with me every minute until I leave."

78

"Well, maybe I can. Henri gave me tomorrow off and then I have my regular two days off. If you'll have me, I'm yours for the next three days. I can go with you wherever you're going tomorrow. I don't know how, but maybe I can help you."

They walked into her cottage, Jordan's arm tightly wrapped around her waist. As soon as they got inside he pulled her to him and kissed her again. "Careful, Jordan, if you keep that up the coq au vin will burn, and you'll be looking at a blackened mess for dinner."

"Turn the oven down to warm. Dinner can wait. I can't."

He led her into the bedroom and sat down on the edge of the bed, pulling her to him. He laid down on it, bringing her with him. She slowly reached down and unzipped his pants, freeing his erect penis and began to slide her hand up and down his shaft as he moaned with pleasure. His hands were shaking with desire as she helped him take her jeans off. He couldn't hold back and entered her. She came as quickly as he did.

"God, I'm sorry. I've been thinking about you all day. I just couldn't help myself. I promise you I'll be a better lover next time. Actually, I want to please you as much as I like being pleased. That's a very new feeling for me. I've always enjoyed women, but when I'm with you, I'm on a completely different level. We've only known each other a little over two days, and I'm beginning to wonder if I haven't been really lonely, and all the women, wine, and gourmet meals were just compensating for it. Thank you for giving yourself fully and totally to me."

"Hush," she said, gently kissing him. "Believe me when I tell you that you please me as much as I hope I please you."

She was a joyful, spontaneous lover, unashamed of her body, and eager to please him. Making love with Elena was the easiest, most joyful thing in the world. The thought of leaving her was becoming more difficult with each passing hour. They were both tired and soon fell into a short post-lovemaking nap, waking refreshed and hungry.

"Why don't you shower and by the time you're finished, dinner will be on the table. All I need to do is turn the oven up and sauté some vegetables. I've already made the salad. I just have to blend the vinaigrette for it. It won't take long." She quickly dressed and walked into the kitchen.

"My God, what do I smell? Whatever it is, it's fantastic," Jordan said as he walked into the kitchen few minutes later.

"Well, it could be me, but you're probably used to that smell by now. It could be the coq au vin, or the garlic I sautéed with the vegetables. Please sit down and start eating. When you're ready, tell me what happened today. I've been so curious."

"I found two more paintings, but more importantly, I found out that the name of the chef is Pierre Yount. But I've hit a snag. I really thought Pierre was the only person I needed to find. I discovered a Donna Shuster painting in a gallery and showed Pierre's picture to the owner, but he was quite guarded and very antagonistic. He obviously didn't want to talk to me, and said that the man in the photograph was definitely not the man who sold him the painting."

"Wait a minute," she said. "If that's true, that means Pierre has an accomplice or that Pierre is the other man's accomplice. Is that right?"

"Yes. I not only need to find Pierre, but it looks like I also need to find this other man, whoever he is. Elena, excuse me," he said, pushing back his chair. "I want to get Pierre's picture from my sling bag and have you look at it. I meant to show you last night, but I got sidetracked. He may have eaten at Henri's. I'll be right back."

When he returned, he opened his bag and took out the photograph. "Do you recognize this man?" he asked. She glanced at the photograph and immediately looked up at him.

"Yes, He came to Henri's for lunch, liked my beef bourguignon and asked to meet me, much as you did. I don't think he ever told me his name even though we talked for a long time. He even came back the next day. As I remember, he has a tattoo of a chef's knife on his arm. He told me he lives in California, and was in Provence visiting his family who lives in the Avignon area. He said his parents are aging, and that he tries to come back to France several times a year to see them. I remember he also said that he sends money to help them now that his father can no longer work."

"Are you certain about this?" he said, sitting down once again and taking a bite of the coq-au-vin. "By the way, this is the best I've ever had and I'm a connoisseur of this dish. Even the vegetables are cooked perfectly."

"I'm glad you like it, but back to Pierre. I remember the conversation vividly. I asked him if he was a chef in California. He said he'd worked in several restaurants, but that one of his customers, a very wealthy female businesswoman, had asked him to be her private chef, and now Pierre travels all over the world with her in her private jet. His employer will only eat meals that Pierre prepares. Does that help?"

"You've just saved me hours of work and investigation. Excuse me. I need to email Chief Lewis about this. Please, continue to eat. I'll only be a minute." He took two steps and paused, turning back to her. "Don't eat all of it. I want another serving when I get back."

He took his phone out of his sling bag and spent several minutes typing an email message. Almost immediately, he felt a vibration coming from it, indicating he had a phone call. He looked at the screen and saw it was Chief Lewis.

"Good morning, Chief. I know it's almost lunch time in Southern California, but I thought you'd want to know what I've found out. There's a woman I've met, Elena Johnson, and she confirmed that the name of the man I sent you the picture of is Pierre Yount." Jordan paused. "Yes, yes. I can go there tomorrow." He was quiet, listening. "Yes, she can come with me. She's already been a huge help to me and her French is far better than mine. I'll try and email you when we return.

"By the way, can you have someone check on French law regarding returning these paintings to the United States? I understand that the Laguna Beach gallery's insurance company paid them for the loss they incurred in the burglary and that any legal action in civil court to recover possession of the stolen paintings would have to be taken by the insurance company that paid the claim."

82

He put his hand over the phone and whispered to Elena, "Would you hand me my wine? Thanks." He paused for a moment, taking a sip of the wine.

Jordan continued, "I remember a couple of cases several years ago when France refused the request of a California insurance company to return stolen paintings which had been sold to gallery owners in France. They felt that the French gallery owners would suffer huge financial losses if they had to give up the paintings because they unknowingly had purchased what turned out to be stolen paintings. I recall the insurance company had no recourse if France didn't cooperate because our legal authority ends at the American border.

"Lastly, and probably most difficult, is there any way to find out which wealthy entrepreneurs have private chefs? I'm beginning to think we aren't going to have any luck with the French authorities, but if we could find Pierre Yount in California, and if he had stolen property on him, maybe we could arrest him. Of course, that doesn't help with the accomplice.

"Oh, and Chief, it's a well-known fact that very haphazard customs searches are conducted on people who land in private planes, particularly if they're well-known. Maybe that's how Pierre got these paintings smuggled into France. And if that's so, he may be smuggling other items into other countries and selling them to unsuspecting galleries as well. Just a thought."

After he ended the call, he turned to Elena. "I'd like you to go with me to Avignon and Aix tomorrow. There are a couple of galleries in both of those towns. I'd also like to get more information on where Pierre's parents live. Both you and one of the chefs I talked to said that he has family in the area. If we find them, you could tell them that you need to get in touch with him. You could say you're thinking of moving to California, and Pierre told you that he could help you find work there. Who knows, it might work."

"Yes. I can do that."

He grinned at her. "Oh, by the way, I'm spending the night. My suitcase is in the trunk of the car. I checked out of Chateau Pascal. I told you I want to be with you every minute the rest of the time I'm here. This may not help you with those gossipy women from the village, but I don't give a damn."

Elena just looked at him as he sat across the table from her. She wondered what would happen if she told him the truth about her past. Would he leave immediately?

Well, there's no reason to tell him. He'll be gone in a few days and I'll have these memories to sustain me for the rest of my life.

"I'm so glad you're staying tonight. I was lonesome when you left last night, and I missed you today. I know we only have a short time left and I'm prepared for that, but I'm going to treasure every hour I have with you. Thank you." She got up and walked around the table, bending down to kiss him.

They made plans for the next day. Avignon was a large town for the region, with a population of nearly 100,000 and Jordan was able to locate several art galleries in it. He also mapped out several of the top restaurants. Even though they could only eat in one or two, they might be able to find something out from chefs who worked in the other restaurants.

Avignon seemed like the logical place to start and then they could travel south to Aix-en-Provence, an even larger town which was the home of a well-known university. They planned on spending as much time as needed in both towns.

They were tired and ready for bed, but sleep came later. For a long time Jordan laid next to Elena, listening to her soft breathing. He wondered how she would fit into his life if he asked her to come with him to California. For the first time in his life, he wanted to live with a woman. He knew he had his shortcomings and could be overbearing and impatient, but she brought out the best in him. However, she seemed to be carrying a secret. There was some reason why she didn't want to go back to the United States, and even after spending intimate time with her, she hadn't told him. He was a man who was used to finding out things, but he certainly hadn't been successful with her.

What could it be? What could have happened in the United States that would cause her to live the life of a reclusive expat, albeit a very beautiful one?

No answers came to him and he finally fell asleep, dreaming of paintings, food, and perhaps more of Elena in the middle of the night.

CHAPTER 14

In the morning, they leisurely dressed. Jordan wore frayed jeans and a jacket with leather elbow patches. The jacket concealed his gun. He decided to disguise himself with an applied mustache and goatee. For her part, Elena had pulled her hair severely away from her face and held it in place with a simple barrette. She wore no make-up. A cloth hobo bag, black boots, a navy blue sweater, and jeans completed her outfit. Anyone looking at them would assume they were professors from the university at either Avignon or Aix.

They left her cottage about 8:30 a.m. on their way to have coffee and a croissant at Le Zeste, planning on touring the galleries afterwards. The restaurant was crowded, and by the time they finished, the galleries were open. Fortunately, all of them were located nearby.

Although they were able to visit four of the galleries before they closed at noon, they had no luck. The galleries were larger than the other ones Jordan had visited, and with Avignon being a well-known tourist town, the art they saw was definitely geared more to the tourist trade than to fine art collectors.

"We're drawing a big zero. Let's go to a couple of restaurants and see if we can find waiters or chefs who might know Pierre. The Collection Lambert Hotel is nearby. It has a number of art exhibits and supposedly a very fine restaurant. Let's start there," Jordan said.

They wandered through several of the exhibits, ending up at the Metropolitan Restaurant. While they were sharing a salad and enjoying a glass of wine, Elena suddenly blurted out, "I don't think we're going to find the last two pieces in Avignon. If Pierre and his family are from this area, as we've been told, he could easily be recognized, and questions would be raised as to why he was selling American art when he returned home. He's a chef, not an art dealer. I think we need to start showing the photograph of him to people who work in restaurants, and see if we can locate his family."

Jordan thoughtfully sipped his wine. "I think you're absolutely right. If we can find his family, they may be able to help us. Let's start. *Monsieur*," he said, waving the waiter over to their table, "Do you know the man in this photograph?"

"*Oui, c'est Monsieur* Yount. He always comes here to eat when he returns to Avignon."

Jordan could feel butterflies in his stomach. He knew they were close to fitting some of the missing puzzle pieces together. "Do you know where his family lives?"

"No, *Monsieur*. I'll go ask our chef. He might be able to help. He's been here a long time. May I take the photograph with me?" he asked.

He took the photo from Jordan and walked through the doors that led to a large kitchen. A few minutes later a large man wearing a tall, white chef's hat with a spattered half-apron tied around his waist, walked over to their table. His grey-hair was neatly tied in a ponytail at the nape of his neck.

"May I help you?" he asked. "Antoine told me that you asked about Pierre. He is a friend of mine. Why do you want to find him or his family?"

Although the chef was not belligerent, it was very clear from his tone that Jordan better have a very good answer, or there would be no information coming from him.

"He told *Mademoiselle* that he would help her get a job as a chef at a restaurant in California. He said he would return to the restaurant where she works in St. Victor la Coste the following day, but he never came back. He mentioned that his parents lived in the Avignon area, and she thought maybe someone here would know how she could get in touch with him or his family," Jordan lied.

They both looked at the chef who was shifting his weight from one foot to the other while he stared at the photograph. He appeared to be having a hard time deciding whether or not to tell them anything about Pierre. He looked up from the photograph and looked at each of them for what seemed like minutes.

Finally, he said, "I've been to his family's home, but it was many years ago. You might ask Chef Bernard at the restaurant *Ginette et Marcel,* which is located just down the street. It's also *un épicier,* and I know Pierre always frequents it when he comes back. You can easily walk to it."

"*Merci beaucoup, Monsieur*, you've been most helpful. We'll go there now." They paid and left. The restaurant was only a short walk away.

Everywhere they looked, the past was evident. Elena had lived in Provence for only six months, but she'd spent a lot of time reading about the area, and particularly about Avignon, one of the largest cities in the region.

"Jordan, I was raised in a very strong Catholic household. I haven't been to church for some time and now I consider myself to be a lapsed Catholic. I remember learning years ago that Avignon was the seat of the papacy in the 14th century. Pope Clement V, a Frenchman, refused to move to Rome when he became the pope. For sixty-seven years there was a papal community in Avignon, and even today there are numerous minor churches in the town. The two best known ones are the *Palais des Papes* and the *Notre Dame de Doms*. Both of them overlook the city and they're a 'must see' on every tourist's list."

As they slowly walked to the restaurant, Elena continued, "Did you know that the Avignon was considered to be the seat of culture in the area?" She made a broad gesture and pointed to the *Palais des Papes*. "That's where they have the traditional plays, but there's also a more bohemian "Festival Off..."

He stopped walking and turned to face her. "A Festival Off? What the hell is that?"

"That's where they showcase undiscovered plays and street performers. Anyway, that's what it says at the bottom of the city map. Plus, and you'll love this, Jordan, Avignon is widely known for its art and many fine restaurants. And so ends my travelogue! Don't you feel enlightened?" she asked, as they resumed walking.

"Not particularly, but just talking about the restaurants makes me hungry again. When I get back to California, I'm going to have to spend some serious time running on the beach to work off all this wine and fabulous food."

89

When they got to *Ginette et Marcel* it was nearly 1:00 p.m. and packed with a hungry lunch crowd.

"*Mademoiselle*," Jordan said to the hostess, "We are trying to locate the man in this photograph and we were referred to this restaurant. His name is Pierre Yount. We were told that Chef Bernard might know him. May we speak with him for a moment?"

Looking out at the patio, they could see that every table was taken, and from the number of people standing around, it looked like there would be a long wait. The pretty dark-haired hostess was extremely gracious. "Chef Bernard is taking a break behind the restaurant in the garden area. He does like his cigarettes and finds time to sneak one every hour or so. Come with me."

They followed her through the kitchen and out the back door. Someone with a very green thumb had been carefully tending the raised planters, which were bursting with ripe vegetables and herbs.

"Chef, I'm sorry to bother you, but these people are looking for a man they have been told might be a friend of yours, *Monsieur* Pierre Yount." She turned to Elena and Jordan, "Excuse me. I must get back to the front desk." She walked back through the kitchen door.

Standing in front of Jordan with a cigarette hanging from his lips was one of the largest men Jordan had ever seen. Jordan was 6'2," but Chef Bernard towered over him. He wore a splotchy apron over his large belly, which clearly showed the remnants of the day's breakfasts and lunches.

Jordan introduced himself and Elena to the chef. "*Madamoiselle* Johnson and I are looking for Pierre Yount. He promised to help her find a job in California. Do you know where his parents live? We hope to find them and maybe they can tell *Mademoiselle* how she might get in touch with him."

Chef Bernard paused thoughtfully as he looked them over, and then began to speak. "I have not seen Pierre for several months. His parents live in Travaillan, a small village on the outskirts of Orange. His father was a hunting guide before he had a bad accident and had to stop guiding. They are very poor, and I know Pierre helps them out whenever he can. If you're going there, let me pack some food for them. I'm told they often have a large number of people staying at their home."

He stubbed his cigarette out in a large ashtray set on an old tree stump. "Sit down. I'll be back shortly." Several minutes later he returned with two large bags filled with food.

"They know me. Tell them I'll visit soon. When you get to the village of Travaillan, drive through it and then at the third stop sign, turn right. The road winds and up about a half mile, you'll see a run-down house with chickens in the yard. There will also probably be a pig or two and some old rusted appliances. They're good people." He turned around and went back into the kitchen.

Jordan and Elena let themselves out the back gate, each carrying a heavy bag loaded with food. Elena briefly regretted that she hadn't ordered the *chevre miel tartine*, the open-faced goat cheese and honey sandwich that she'd seen on the serving counter in the kitchen. She decided to make it herself within the next couple of days.

"Elena, did you hear him mention something about several people living or staying with the Younts? I wonder what that's all about."

"I have no idea. Maybe we'll find out when we get there."

PART TWO

KABUL, AFGHANISTAN   APRIL, 2007

CHAPTER 15

"Mike, I'll take it in from here. I've landed in Kabul so many times, I know this air strip like the back of my hand," Darya said. She knew a lot of pilots didn't like landing there because the city was located in a narrow valley, wedged between the Hinju Kush Mountains along the Kabul River.

He stood up, took off his headset and handed it to Darya. She slipped into the pilot's seat and prepared to land the Gulfstream G550. Every time she sat down in the soft leather pilot's seat, she knew she'd made the right decision when she bought it. It was the Cadillac of private business jets, expensive but well worth it. She traveled constantly and often with several members of her staff, so its ability to seat 15 passengers had made it very desirable. Since most of her travels now involved international flights, the plane's range of 6,750 miles was perfect for her needs.

Darya became interested in flying when she was in college and had joined a flying club. She started out learning how to fly small planes and eventually bought a Cessna 172S Skyhawk SP which she used on domestic business flights. She knew one day she wanted to own a plane she could use for international meetings and had spent over a year learning how to fly the Gulfstream.

COYOTE IN PROVENCE

Mike had flown the plane to Afghanistan while she worked at her desk. It was just before sunset and she knew the muezzin would be calling the faithful to evening prayers through the outdoor loudspeakers mounted on the tallest minarets of the mosques. The sounds of the loudspeakers overlapped one another and the descending jet went unnoticed. This was the time of day that she preferred to land. As she began the plane's descent, she could see the brightly colored minarets rising from the mosques forming a skyline of their own as the sky shifted from fading pinks to the light blues of sunset.

The large plane taxied up to the Afghan Immigration and Customs Office outbuilding located near the end of the runway. Private jet passengers were routinely afforded quick entry into the country. She put on her burkha, walked down the plane's stairs, and entered the building. She was followed by Lou, her principal bodyguard, Tela, her secretary, and Pierre, her chef. They traveled with her wherever she went.

Mike would follow after he secured the plane. A few minutes later, the group, having quickly passed through immigration and customs, got into a waiting limousine. They eased into the flow of traffic, preparing for the inevitable checkpoints.

It was only twenty minutes to the Kabul Serena Hotel. She hated the ride through the city. The streets were littered with refuse and in complete disrepair. It used to be that just the homeless were beggars; now small children were everywhere, pleading for food or money. In every direction, there were signs of unrest.

When they arrived at the hotel, they sat down on luxurious couches in the reservation area and waited while Tela

94

took care of the details of getting them registered as guests at the hotel. Darya, Lou, and Tela would stay in the presidential suite and the adjoining executive suite. Mike and Pierre had their own rooms.

"I'm sure you're all tired. Tela, let Mike know he's free for two days. Pierre, I'll see you in the morning at breakfast. Tela has set up a number of appointments for me over the next two days, so I'm going to be quite busy. Enjoy your evening."

"Tela," she said as the bell captain opened the door to the presidential suite, "I'm going to have dinner with some members of my family. Please arrange for a limousine to pick me up in about thirty minutes. Lou," she said to her bodyguard, "You'll come with me to my aunt's home."

She got her cell phone out of her purse and called her aunt, telling her she'd arrived and that she'd be at the family compound in about an hour.

CHAPTER 16

Darya and Lou stepped into the waiting limousine in front of the hotel. The limousine service catered to the wealthy and those who were in need of the latest in protective gear. Tinted bulletproof glass and expert drivers armed with automatic weapons were only a few of the things the prestigious limousine service provided. Security in Afghanistan was always tricky, but at least the passengers felt as safe as was possible.

The driver expertly wove his way through pedestrians, animals, and traffic on his way to the compound in the wealthy Share Naw district of Kabul. Even though she'd left Kabul in 1986, every time Darya returned to Afghanistan, she gave thanks to Allah that her parents had been able to move to the United States.

The sleek black Mercedes pulled up to the gate of the kala. The guard remembered Darya from previous visits and waved the limo into the compound where several large homes surrounded a central parking area. It still unsettled her to see men with automatic weapons patrolling the compound, both within and outside the walls. The door to the largest house opened and Darya's aunt, Husna, came out the door to greet her.

Darya quickly opened the car door before the driver or Lou had a chance to assist her and greeted her aunt in a shared hug, both saying *Salaam* at the same time.

"Come, you must be tired," Husna said. "We will have tea."

The younger sister of her father had always been considered a beauty, but Darya thought she look tired and much older than she remembered. A devout Muslim, she wore a burka even in her home. Although some Afghans made their own wine and drank it before and during dinner as Westerners did, Darya knew no wine would ever be served in this home. She also knew pork would not be on the menu in accordance with the Koran.

Even though Husna was fluent in English, they spoke to each other in Pashto, the national language of Afghanistan, while they drank tea and helped themselves to the grapes and figs that were in a dish that had been placed on a large brass table by servants. After a while, a servant announced that the evening meal was served.

They walked into a room which was large enough to accommodate the extended family while they ate their meals. In keeping with tradition, Darya knew they'd be sitting on the floor to eat. A plastic tablecloth had been placed on the rug with brightly colored cushions surrounding it. The large family soon filled the room.

Salaam, salaam, her cousins said in greeting as they and their children piled onto the cushions that had been placed on the floor. Husna and Haji's children and their grandchildren partially made up the large family. There were also some parents of their children's spouses, bringing the total to over forty people residing in the compound.

The last to enter the room was Haji, Darya's uncle and Husna's husband. He was the head male of the family and his word was law. One of the children carried a copper basin and an elaborately decorated pot filled with water for each member to use to wash their hands. In this compound, nothing had changed for centuries.

Haji greeted Darya in the traditional manner. *"Salaam"* he said, shaking her hand. He sat down on the cushion reserved for him, looking around to make sure that all of the family was present. It was unnecessary as everyone from the smallest baby to Husna would always be where they were expected to be and do what they were expected to do. No one did anything to offend Haji. His autocratic rule of his family was legendary and yet was typical of most Afghan families.

Servants brought in one dish after another: grilled lamb kebabs; Afghanistan's national dish, *quabili palao* with meat and stock topped with fried raisins, slivered carrots and pistachios; rice with meatballs; dumplings; tandoori chicken; salad; *naan* and *lavash* breads; an onion based stew with beef, yogurt and spices; and stuffed grape leaves. Chutney and pickled fruits accompanied the dishes with dessert consisting of *gosh e feel*, thin fried pastries covered with powdered sugar and ground pistachios. They ate communal style, passing the food and eating with their fingers of their right hand. Each time a platter was empty another dish quickly replaced it. Darya knew this was one place she didn't need to have her food tested for poisonous substances.

After dinner everyone left for their respective homes located within the compound and Haji went into his office. Husna and Darya sat and talked. Soon all of the dishes had been cleared and they were the only ones in the room. Darya's aunt began to speak.

"Darya, there are things I must tell you. I have cancer and not long to live."

"No, that can't be!" Darya exclaimed, her hand unconsciously rising to her chest as if to ward off the thought. "You look so good. Surely there's a mistake. What makes you think that?"

"Three doctors have told me I have a type of cancer that is incurable. No, don't cry," she said as she leaned over and brushed a tear from Darya's cheek. "I have made my peace with Allah. Haji knows but refuses to accept it. He even had me flown to Paris in hopes a doctor there could help. That specialist told me the same thing. It is inoperable and incurable. Haji prays to Allah for me to be cured, but it's no use. I need you to do something for me, but no one must know about it. It is really important to me. Will you?"

"Of course, Husna, whatever you need. Would you like to come to the United States and see doctors there? Father still teaches at Harvard and knows many doctors."

"No, Darya, this has nothing to do with my health. Just listen to me and don't interrupt. When I was married my mother gave me a great deal of jewelry that had been in our family for many generations. I was her only daughter. She told she knew I was marrying a wealthy man, but there may come a time when I would need it. That time has arrived."

"Husna, I'm sorry to interrupt, but does my father know about your health? He has said nothing to me."

"No. Please, just listen to me. You know that Haji is a very wealthy businessman. Do you know where that wealth comes from?"

Darya took a deep breath and looked fully at her aunt before she answered. "I am sorry to say this, but I have heard rumors that although he has many legitimate businesses, most of his wealth comes from the opium trade."

"Yes, the rumors are true. In fact, the opium production is at a record high level this year. I didn't know about it when I married him and when I found out about it, it was too late for me to do anything, not that I could have anyway. I love Haji very much and he loves me. Our marriage was arranged and I was only fifteen years old when I married him. He treats me well. He has never laid a hand on me, which, as you know, is very rare in our country. Haji even insisted I become educated and had college professors come to the house to teach me.

"And something else. My mother would not allow my clitoris to be removed when I was born, even though it was traditional among the Muslim faithful in this country. Haji accepted that and even supported me when I refused to allow our daughters be victims of female genital mutilation."

"I am very much aware of the practice of female genital mutilation in the Afghan society," Darya responded. In fact, I did my master's thesis on it and even wrote a book about it, which by the way, was not well received in this country. It's a barbaric practice that must be stopped."

"Yes," Husna said. "But it's still done in almost all of the traditional Muslim homes. Our country, as well as our religion, is ruled by men and for centuries, it has been associated with female sexual purity. But that's not the reason I wanted to talk to you, although I hope it shows you that your uncle is a good man. I have seen what opium does to people and while I can't do anything about his involvement, I have been doing something that makes me feel a little better about my life."

"What is that? It sounds very intriguing, whatever it is."

Husna looked around to see if anyone had entered the room while they had been talking. The servants were in the kitchen, cleaning up from the meal. She leaned forward, getting closer to Darya.

"For the last year I have been paying to support an orphanage on the outskirts of town. My driver's family finds young girls, usually on the streets of Kabul, and takes them there. He sells my jewelry to pay for their care at the orphanage. No one knows, not even my daughters. These little girls will break your heart. They have been badly abused and some of them have even been tortured. Their parents put them on the streets because they couldn't feed them, or because they were girls, or they're orphans because their parents have been killed in the war. It is so sad. Why Allah allows this, I don't know."

"You must have people who live there and take care of the girls. How many of them are there?"

"Right now there are around fifteen, but it varies. Some of them die from the abuse they have suffered. There is a little graveyard behind the building. No one would claim the bodies anyway. Haji is leaving on a business trip tomorrow and will be gone for several days. I would like you to come back here tomorrow and my driver will take us to the orphanage. Because of my failing health, I won't be able to go out of the house much longer. The pain is getting very bad. Please Darya, I need your help. Can you come tomorrow?"

"Yes. I will find a way to do this for you, no matter what appointments I have to cancel. What time do you want me here?"

"The little girls take naps in the afternoon. I'd rather you see them when they are active. Come around ten in the morning. It shouldn't take more than two hours. Now it's time for you to go. My strength is leaving and I don't want you to see me like that. Until tomorrow," she said, grimacing in pain.

She rang a bell and immediately a large woman stepped into the room. "Fahima, I am ready to go to my room. Please help me." The strong woman supported her as she stood up.

Darya went into the nearby room to get Lou. "I'm ready to go. Please call the driver and tell him we will be waiting for him at the front door."

The drive back to the hotel from her aunt's home seemed much longer to Darya. She was still trying to absorb everything her aunt had told her and having a difficult time doing it. She didn't know how she was going to be able to talk with her parents and not tell them.

When she got back in her hotel suite, she told Tela that she would have to represent her at the morning meetings scheduled for the next day; that she had pressing family business which took priority.

Her mind was whirling as she got in bed. After a sleepless hour, she got out of bed and found the sleeping pills the doctor had prescribed for her many months ago. Although she took them with her when she traveled, she'd never needed them before. Given everything that had happened tonight and not knowing what to expect tomorrow, she was glad she'd thought to bring them.

CHAPTER 17

The next morning Darya got into the limousine feeling rested after a good night's sleep. As was always the case when Darya traveled overseas, Lou accompanied her. He was her senior bodyguard. When they returned to California, one of her other bodyguards would accompany her, giving Lou some time off.

She looked out the window of the limousine and what she saw reminded her of news reports she'd seen of war-torn third world countries. She was well aware of the toll the years of unrest had taken on the city, but in the light of day it was even more horrific than what she had seen last night. Every time she came back, it seemed to have regressed another hundred years.

Her reverie was broken by the uniformed armed guard motioning her driver into the compound. She told him to pull over to the side of the large parking area and wait there until she returned. Her aunt and her driver were already in her aunt's car waiting for Darya.

"I'm sorry Husna, but I need to bring my bodyguard with me."

"Of course. That will be fine. We have plenty of room. This is my driver, Gul. I have no secrets from him and he is to be trusted."

Gul drove eastward. The farther they got from the wealthy district where her aunt lived, the more appalling the living conditions. Tent camps and shanties made of nothing more than tar paper held together with salvaged lumber stood side by side. Dust swirled everywhere. It looked like something out of a dystopian novel. Darya shook her head, not believing the depth of the abject poverty and suffering she was witnessing.

Darya knew that the wealthy transferred a lot of their money out of Afghanistan. Even her aunt and uncle had recently bought a large home in Dubai. This was a country where the "haves" were very wealthy and the "have-nots" were beyond poor, simply existing from day to day.

Gul spoke to her aunt in rapid Pashto as they pulled off the road onto a dirt track. Just ahead in the swirling dust, Darya could see a flat-roofed mud house with a wing on each side of the central part of the building. Gul pulled up to the front door and stopped the car. Lou got out and opened the back door. "Wait," Husna said, "Gul thinks it would be better if your guard stayed in the car. He's afraid he will scare the little girls. There is nothing to fear here. Gul will be with us and he is armed. You will be safe."

"Yes, that will be fine with me."

The door to the mud house was opened by an elderly Muslim woman just as Gul prepared to knock. She motioned for them to enter.

"Husna," Darya said, "how often do you come? She doesn't seem to know you."

"This is only my second time. I can't risk having Haji find out about it."

105

Nothing in Darya's life prepared her for what she saw when she stepped through the door. There were about fifteen young girls assembled in a large open room. All of them had suffered horrible physical losses. Many of them were missing limbs and eyes. Burns and scars were the norm. Darya felt warm tears in her eyes and fought the nausea that rose in her throat.

"Husna, this is far beyond what you told me. These children are filthy. They have caked mud on them and open running sores. Is there no medical care for them here?"

"You speak like someone from the United States. There is no running water here or electricity. The two women Gul hired are family members of his. It is very difficult for them to get water from the well for cooking and drinking, much less cleaning the girls up. Because they are only girls, a place like this would never be allowed in the parts of Kabul that have utility services."

"But Husna, how will they ever heal without medical treatment and things like clean running water?"

"Right now we are trying to keep them alive by feeding them. That's about all we can do. I am happy they are off the streets, but so much more needs to be done. We'll talk more about them when we get back to my house."

Darya, Gul and Husna toured the house, Gul doing the talking. With their burkhas and veils, Darya and Husna were unrecognizable. He told the women working there that Darya and Husna were rich benefactors who might want to help. There was a large room in the center of the house where the girls spent most of their time. A fire pit was in back of the house where the cooking was done. On either side of the main room were large

106

rooms with filthy mattresses covering the floor. An outhouse was located a few yards from the back of the house. That was it. No washer, no dryer, no refrigerator, no stove and no bathroom with a toilet and sink. This was a house where the only thing that mattered was survival.

On the drive back to the compound, everyone was silent. Darya was having trouble processing what she had just seen. She wasn't ready to talk about it in front of Lou. Although she trusted him with her life, literally, he was only human. If it were known that the wife of Haji Massoud was sponsoring an orphanage for little girls, that knowledge could be worth a lot of money, most likely as blackmail paid by Haji. Even though Lou was an American, and a trusted member of her staff, she thought it best not to speak about what she had seen in his presence.

After they returned to the compound, Darya told Lou to go into a nearby room while she spoke with her aunt. She joined her aunt in the small room off of the main hall and was surprised to see Gul there as well. Domestic help and family members rarely mingle in Afghanistan.

"Sit down, Darya. I am very tired, so this will be short. I can see that you're surprised that I invited Gul to join us. It's essential that you two know one another. The doctors have given me another month or two, at best. I know better. My time here is coming to an end." She stopped and took a drink of water from a glass at her side.

"Darya, I want this to be my legacy even though no one here will know about it. You have a plane and you are a pilot. Immigration and customs officials here are paid off regularly for all kinds of things. If they were paid well, they would not notice the little girls.

107

"Gul and I have done some research. His nephew is very good with a computer. We've learned that there are private airports people can fly into in various parts of the world where immigrations and customs inspections are barely conducted. If these people were given money, they might overlook little girls. My dream is to get them to the United States and have them adopted. Of course, they would need some form of ID. That is my dream, Darya. Now I need you to go. I am very tired. Think about what I have said. When will you be back here?"

"I am planning to return in two weeks. I will come and see you then. Take care of yourself. May I please tell my parents about your medical condition?"

"No, they would want to come and see me one more time. It will be better when I am gone. I will see you in two weeks." She rang the bell and immediately Fahima was at her side. Darya watched her leave, feeling as if her heart was being tightly squeezed.

What a brave, wonderful woman. I have no idea how I'm going to do this, but I will. I will do it for her.

"Gul, my aunt said that your nephew is a computer whiz. I am quite comfortable with the computer. I think it would be a good idea for you and me to make plans through him. Can you do that?"

"Yes. Here is how to reach him. He has a computer in his house, but it doesn't always work. He lives next door to me. Your aunt is a wonderful woman. Every person who works here loves her. We will take care of her. Don't worry."

She looked at her watch as her phone rang. "Yes, Tela, I am on my way. I will be going to the afternoon meetings. You can fill me in later. Thanks for attending the morning meetings in my place."

Darya was physically present at the afternoon meetings, but most of the time her mind was miles away, trying to figure out how she was going to get the little girls to the United States. She'd never encountered a situation like this, in fact, she was sure that very few people had.

Well, when I began my company people laughed at the thought of an Afghan woman as a successful business executive. They're not laughing now. If I did that, I can find a way to get those little girls to the United States.

When they got out of the last meeting she turned to Tela, "Cancel the meetings for tomorrow. I know we have an important dinner meeting tonight, but I want to leave after that. Call Mike and tell him I need to fly to Marseille. I understand that most cities have small airports for private planes. Tell him to find one in the Marseille area that has immigration and customs. That's where I want to land. We'll spend the rest of the night there so make arrangements at a hotel and have a limousine pick us up." Tela was already making calls as they walked to their suite.

CHAPTER 18

The limousine was at the front door of the hotel, ready to take them to the airport when she and Tela returned from the dinner meeting. Tela told her that Mike was already at the airport and that the plane was ready to go. When they got to the airport, they entered the immigration and customs building that serviced private planes. Darya hadn't paid much attention before, but she realized the immigration people who were there this evening were the same ones who had been there when they landed. Thinking about it, she realized that she'd seen the same individuals most of the time she'd taken off and landed in Kabul.

It was quiet in the outbuilding where the offices were located, and no planes were landing or taking off. Darya walked over to the immigration official who appeared to be in charge. "Pardon me, sir, but I have a question."

"Yes, how can I help you?"

"I have some people who would like to get out of Kabul, but they lost their identifications in a bombing. I was wondering if there was anything I could do to help them. I would like to fly them out of here. Can you help me?"

Darya was an expert at reading people and she immediately knew that she was going to be able to get the girls out of Kabul. It was just a matter of how much it would cost her.

"I don't usually do this type of thing, but if the price was right, I might overlook the lack of proper papers," the immigration official said.

"And what would that price be?" she asked.

"How many people are you thinking of flying out of here?"

"About fifteen."

"Let me think." He paused and then said, "I would need 20,000 AFN for each one of them."

She quickly calculated that it would run about $350.00 for each little girl. "All right. I can do that. When are you here?"

"I am off Fridays and Saturdays. I work from 3:00 p.m. to 11:00 p.m."

"Good. I'll see you in about two weeks. Remember our little talk. When I leave I'll have an envelope for you. The money will be in it. Thank you and I look forward to seeing you."

She walked back to her group. "You must have learned some good news," Pierre said, "You're wearing a huge smile."

"Yes. I learned some very good news." She waved at the immigration inspector as her group followed her to the plane, Lou, as always, only a few yards behind her.

As soon as she got in the plane she went into the bathroom and took off her burkha. Her mind was spinning. Now she knew she could get the girls out of Kabul, but where was she going to put them and how was she going to get them into the United States?

About an hour before the scheduled landing in Marseille, the light on the phone next to her seat blinked, indicating that the pilot wanted to talk to her. Even though she had a pilot's license, she usually let Mike fly, Kabul being the exception.

"Miss Rahimi, we will be landing at the airport we usually use. I know you requested a smaller airport, but this one has very little traffic this time of night. It does allow flights in and out and has French Immigration and Customs. I thought it might work well for whatever you need."

"That's fine, Mike. I trust your judgment. Let's see, we're scheduled to land about 6:00 a.m. Marseille time, right?"

"Yes, ma'am. I checked with the tower and no other flights are scheduled to land or take off for the next hour. We should be able to get through there easily."

As she hung up the phone, Pierre made his way over to her seat. "Miss Rahimi, how long do you plan on being in Marseille? I'm wondering if there will be enough time for me to take a short trip to see my parents."

She thought a minute. "Yes. I'd like to go with you. I've never met your parents. You've told me how beautiful that part of Provence is and I'd like to see it. We'll take a limousine."

"Well," Pierre said, "that will be a first. I doubt that my parents have ever seen a limousine. Maybe we could take them for a little drive in it. I'm sure they'd like that."

"For what the limousine service charges me, it won't be a problem if you want to take them for a ride. Mike told me we should be there in an hour. You can email them. You know we have Wi-Fi on the plane."

"You have not met my parents. I don't think they've even heard of the Internet. A rotary phone is as modern as they're ever going to be. Maman still hangs her clothes out to dry on an outdoor clothes line."

"And they probably smell a lot better than my satin sheets," Darya said, smiling at the charming image in her mind of an old lady hanging up wash in the countryside.

"I'll call them later and tell them I will be visiting them early this morning. The roosters wake them up at dawn so that shouldn't be a problem. I think it's better if I don't mention you. They would work too hard trying to make things look good for you."

An hour later Mike expertly landed the plane at Marseille and taxied up to the small building that housed French Immigration and Customs. The front porch light was on as well as lights inside. They got their luggage out of the plane and walked into the building. They could see a limousine waiting for them on the other side of the building.

"Go ahead," Darya said, "I want to talk to the inspector when all of you are finished. I'm going to be coming here often in the next few months and I want to ask him some questions. You can wait for me in the limo."

Her group easily made it through immigration and customs. All of them were used to traveling with Darya and knew this was just part of their job. When it was her turn, Darya showed the inspector her United States passport. While she'd been waiting, she'd noticed a photograph of a woman and two little girls on his desk.

"Excuse me, I couldn't help but notice your photo of a woman and two little girls. Is that your family?"

"Yes. They don't like it when I have to be away from them at night. I work three nights and two days. The days are much better."

"Does your wife work outside of the home? I don't know whether it is common for women to do that in Marseille."

"No, sometimes I wish she did. We could use the money, but we both feel it's more important for her to be at home with the girls, particularly with my schedule. It's better for them."

"If you would like to make a little more money, I might be able to help you."

He looked at her. "I won't do anything illegal. If you're thinking about bringing in drugs or guns, *non*. My girls are more important to me than some extra money. What would they do if something happened to me?"

"What I'm asking you to do doesn't involve drugs or guns. I would like to bring some Afghan orphans into Marseille. I need to get medical care for them and see that they are well taken care of. Then I'd like to fly them to the United States where they can be adopted. I could really use your help. Without your help, I don't know what will happen to them. Some of their families have abandoned them and some have parents that have been killed in the war. They're missing arms and legs. Several have been beaten or scarred from knives and cigarettes. Here are some photos I took of them." She handed him her cell phone.

As he looked at the photos, his face became ashen and his bushy black eyebrows rose in disbelief. "*Mon Dieu*," he said as he crossed himself, "You are speaking the truth?"

"Yes. There is a small orphanage outside of Kabul with no running water or electricity, but the girls are better off there than on the streets of Kabul. They are filthy, need medical attention, and are suffering from malnutrition. When I saw them, I wanted to help. I'm just now making plans. Will you help me?" she asked.

"*Oui.*"

"What will you charge me?"

He stroked his chin with his long fingers as he thought about it. "Is this only once, or will you be doing this often?"

"I'm not sure. I imagine it will be more than once, probably several times a year."

115

He was quiet and then said, "I would like to have two thousand euros each time you land and take off with them. I think that's fair. If anyone finds out about this, I could lose my job."

"All right. Two thousand euros it is. When should I plan on landing or taking off?"

"I work Tuesday, Wednesday and Thursday nights. If you could land around this time, it would be best because there are very few planes taking off or landing and my shift is over at 8:00 a.m. When will you be starting this?"

"I don't know. I need to find somewhere for the girls to stay while they're here and I need to find people to help me in the United States. I will see you in a few weeks. Would you like me to notify you ahead of time?"

"Yes, please. Here is my card. I will write my cell phone number on the back of it."

"Thank you and I look forward to doing business with you," she said as she walked out the door and into the waiting limousine.

She called Mike as she and Pierre drove to Travaillan, the small village near where Pierre's parents lived. "Could we take off tonight? I'm anxious to get back." She listened for a minute. "Yes, I can have everyone at the plane at 7:00 p.m. Are you sure you'll be rested enough? I know there's some pilot directive on this and I don't want to ask you to do something that may cause problems for you." She listened, then said, "I'll have Tela call them and we'll meet   you there. Sleep well."

Later that evening as she walked up the steps of the plane, all she could think about was the orphanage, her aunt, and how she could carry out her promise.

SOUTHERN CALIFORNIA   JUNE, 2006

CHAPTER 19

At 4:30 in the afternoon, Darya was sitting at her desk in her office in Santa Monica when the buzzer on her desk rang. "Yes?" she said into the intercom.

"Miss Rahimi, Slade Kelly is here with two men. Is it alright for me to show them into your office?"

"Yes, Mahsa, that will be fine."

The door opened and Slade and two men walked in. Darya had to hand it to him. True to his word, he'd brought two of his men to work undercover in her company. He was worried that she might be the target of Islamic terrorists.

One of the men looked like a patrician CPA and the other one had a broken nose with red veins, scars on his face and a physique that indicated he'd spent a lot of time working out with weights or lifting heavy loads. He looked like he'd be at home on the docks or in a local dive bar. They were both absolutely perfect for their new assignments.

"Doll, this here's Boris Karpov and this is Andrew Berry. They'll be startin' tomorrow. Just wanted you to meet 'em. I told the HR Supervisor to give notice to them two HR people that wasn't checkin' references. They're cleanin' out their desks as we speak. The head of HR seems OK. She's already posted for two new people. Think reference checkin' gonna be a high priority from now on. Gotta make some calls, but how about we go out to dinner tonight? Friend of mine has a great restaurant not too far from here. Like to get them other two bodyguards to meet you. They was gonna come in this afternoon, but I told 'em to meet us for dinner instead. I'll call and make the reservations seein' how I know the head chef, a guy named Pierre."

She was learning that being with Slade was like riding a roller coaster. Good news one minute and bad news the next. She could only imagine what this restaurant must be like.

"Yes, that would be fine. Let's plan on six o'clock. I have a few things I need to do, but I would like to make it an early night. I think I still have a bit of jet lag. Lou, please let Dave know we'll need him at six. Get the address from Slade and tell him to wait at the restaurant while we have dinner. Thanks."

The limousine was parked directly in front of the reception area, waiting for them. It was a short drive to the restaurant and Slade was feeling good. It had been a very productive day. The limo pulled up in front of a charming Provence style French restaurant complete with a blue door and a riot of flowers tumbling out of pots next to the door.

Interesting. Never would have thought Slade would know the chef at a restaurant that looks like this. This might not be so bad after all.

Two nondescript men were waiting for them in the alcove leading into the restaurant. They followed Slade and Darya as they walked to the maître d's desk. "Slade Kelly, party of five," he said.

"Right this way, sir. Chef Yount said you were to be given the VIP treatment. I hope this table is acceptable to you."

"This is fine, Antoine. When you have a minute, I'd 'preciate it if you would tell Chef Yount that we're here. I'd like to say hello to him."

"Certainly," he said as he pulled a chair out for Darya. "Your waiter will be with you momentarily." Darya was aware that Lou and Slade sat with their backs to the wall so they had an unobstructed view of the restaurant and everyone in it.

The waiter was there in a matter of seconds, handing each one of them black napkins. Although he had both white and black napkins draped over his arm, he deftly matched the black napkin color to what each person was wearing so there would be no hint of white on the men's black slacks or on Darya's black skirt.

He took their drink orders and was back in minutes with Cakebread cabernet sauvignon for Darya, a dirty martini for Slade, a scotch and soda for Jim, vodka tonic for Scott, and a Perrier for Lou, who was technically on duty.

"Jim, Scott, meet your new boss, Darya Rahimi. Lou came aboard last night and he'll be in charge of your schedules. She's high profile 'cause of a book she wrote, plus she's pretty successful. A lot of Muslim men don't look kindly on a woman who's in a place of power. Keep her back covered at all times. This is round the clock and may be for a long time."

"It's nice to meet both of you and I assume we'll become quite close in the future." Darya said, turning to Slade, "Do you really think this will be necessary for a long time, like you just said?"

"Unfortunately, Doll, I think if you wanna stay healthy in the future, not only your health, but your life rests with the people at this table and probably will for a long time. Sorry, sweets, but I didn't write that book. Jim, Scott, Lou, I'm gonna get you a copy of the book Doll wrote. Read it, then you're gonna understan' why some people want her dead."

Darya gulped. It was one thing to have your hotel room tossed, but she'd never thought anyone would want to kill her. Evidently Slade did.

"Okay, guys what's it gonna be? It's on Miss Rahimi tonight, so enjoy."

Darya started to say something, and then thought better of it. After all, dinner was a small price to pay for her life.

"And Doll, I'm gonna write a note to Pierre about your dinner. Want to pull his chain a little. Tell me what you want to eat." The men all ordered steaks, pommes frites, and salads with the house special dressing.

Looking at the menu, Darya said, "Slade, I'd like the baked chicken with the wine sauce, mixed vegetables and the beet and goat cheese salad." Slade wrote her order down on a piece of paper and called Antoine over to the table.

"Waiter took our orders, but I want you to hand-deliver Miss Rahimi's order to Chef Yount. There's some 'structions for him below the order. Thanks," he said as he handed Antoine the note.

In a few minutes the waiter returned with the men's salads. Following him was a large, big-bellied chef wearing black and white checked pants and a white toque, denoting he was the head chef. In his hand was Darya's beet and goat cheese salad.

He put the salad in front of Darya. "Don't eat that yet," Slade said as he got up to hug the chef and made the introductions. "Pierre, you look great. Had to bring these people to your restaurant. Like you to eat a little of Miss Rahimi's salad. Don't scowl at me. I'm the payin' customer here, baby. Just do as I say." He motioned to the waiter to bring an extra salad fork as well as a dinner fork.

With an angry look on his face, Pierre took two bites of the salad, swallowed, and put it back in front of Darya.

"Thanks, Pierre. When our main courses are ready, I want you to bring hers out and taste it. Pierre, quit scowling. Trust me. This may be for your own good."

A few minutes later their salad plates were removed and their main courses were served. As before, Chef Yount followed the server and placed the chicken Darya had ordered in front of her. Frowning the whole time, he took two bites of the chicken and vegetables and returned the plate to the table.

"Mr. Kelly, pardon me, but I have a full house and I need to be get back in the kitchen and do what I'm supposed to be doing, not tasting patrons' food." He turned on his heel and huffed back into the kitchen.

"Well, Doll, how do you like the food?"

"It may be the best I've ever had. Why?"

"Ya need to hire Pierre. Grapevine has it that he's ready for a change and you need a chef. Simple as that. He ain't gonna be cheap, but we go back a long way and he can be trusted. You need people you can trust."

"Well, I've come this far on your recommendations. I might as well do one more. I'll write a note to him. I'm curious. How did you two meet?"

"He was working in one of them fancy Beverly Hills restaurants. Place was packed every night, but somethin' was wrong. It was bleedin' money. The restaurant was owned by some 'vestors and they hired me to figure out why they was losin' money. Turns out the manager had a little problem with drugs. The profits were all going up his nose. Pierre suspected somethin' was wrong and tipped off the 'vestors. We gets together on occasion. He's a good man. Only problem with him is that he wears his heart on his sleeve."

"That's an odd thing to say. What do you mean?"

"He got him some damn good gigs that paid a lot of money. Should be a wealthy man by now, but he's a sucker for any sob story that comes along. Kids and old people do him in. Have as long as I've known him."

123

"Well, I think I like him even better now. Is he always that angry?"

"Naw, I was just pullin' his chain. I mean, what are friends for?"

She called Antoine over and asked him to deliver the note to Pierre she'd written. The phone rang and Antoine spent several minutes telling an angry customer that the restaurant was fully booked and he couldn't possibly accommodate him. While he was talking, Darya signed the credit card slip and the five of them walked out the door to the waiting limousine.

"David, please take Mr. Kelly to the parking lot at the office and then take Lou and me home. Thanks."

"Doll, what'd you put in that note to Pierre?" Slade asked on the short ride to her office.

"I told him I'd like to talk to him and would he please come to my office tomorrow at ten a.m. I'd hoped to get a reply, but Antoine got tied up on the phone. We'll see."

"He'll be there. I want to sit in on the meeting. I'll be there a few minutes before ten. Tell the receptionist and I'll just go on up. Then I want to check on my guys. See you tomorrow, Doll."

The rush hour traffic was over and within just a few minutes Dave pulled the limousine up in front of Darya's condo. It had been a long day, a day in which she'd come face to face with the dangers around her. She shivered and said good night to

Lou as he made his rounds, checking to make sure the condo was secure.

MARCH, 2010

CHAPTER 20

It was after midnight on one of those rare nights in Laguna Beach when you can see the stars. The smog from the inland areas of the Los Angeles basin had been blown out to sea by the Santa Ana winds, leaving the smells of springtime.

The two men were very different in size and shape. One was quite large and portly, the other small and feminine. Each was dressed in black jogging pants and turtlenecks. They wore latex gloves and their faces were covered with wool ski masks. They blended in perfectly with the dark shadows and were nearly invisible as they quietly crept along the alley and stopped at the backdoor that led to the gallery.

Oh merde! Pierre thought. *I should have remembered I'm allergic to wool. Well, I can do anything for a few minutes and that's all the longer this should take. I don't want to sneeze and alert any neighbors who might have a window open or are having one last cigarette.*

Pierre's accomplice placed the duffel bag he was carrying on the ground in front of the gallery's glass door. He reached in the bag and removed a small diamond tipped glass cutting tool and a round suction cup, about the size of a teacup. He attached the suction cup to one of the glass panes in the French door, and then using the glass cutter, made a circular line in the glass around the suction cup.

126

Holding the suction cup in one hand he applied just the right amount of pressure to the glass with his other hand so it wouldn't shatter and make noise. The pane easily broke along the line he'd scored with the glass cutter. With the circular piece of glass still attached to the suction cup, he removed it from the window and quietly placed it on the ground next to the door. He quickly reached through the small hole he'd cut in the glass pane of the door and pressed the button on the door latch that released the lock on the door. To Pierre's jittery nerves, it sounded like a thunderous click which could probably be heard from blocks away.

The small man could feel the sweat running down the back of his neck. He knew that once he opened the gallery door he'd have seven seconds before the alarm would sound and there would also be an automated telephone call to the Laguna Beach police station advising that there had just been an unauthorized entry into the gallery. The police station was located about a mile from the gallery's location. They would only have a few minutes in the gallery before the police would arrive.

In one swift movement he opened the door and entered the gallery. Using his penlight, he dashed into the small office and pulled the lever on the circuit breaker, disabling the alarm without a moment to spare. He held his breath for a moment, wondering if he'd made it in time. He had. The only sound he could hear was the surf breaking on the beach two blocks away.

He motioned to Pierre that it was safe to come into the gallery. The big man entered and quickly took a large mesh bag out of the duffel bag, opening it. He gestured with his free hand for the smaller man to start removing paintings from the wall and put them in the mesh bag as he was doing.

In the distance Pierre thought he could hear the sound of a siren. He cocked his head. No question. It was getting louder and coming in their direction. He grabbed onto the smaller man's arm, almost pushing him out the door. They both hit the alley on the run, Pierre running in one direction and the smaller man in the opposite direction. By prearrangement they'd parked their cars in different locations about two blocks from the gallery and agreed that once they left the gallery, each of them would drive back to their own homes using separate routes. Within minutes they were each in their car, masks and turtlenecks replaced by T-shirts, the seven stolen paintings safely in the trunk of the big man's car.

Pierre started his car and drove the first block with his lights off, trying to avoid detection from neighbors who might have heard him start it. After driving a short distance, he switched on his headlights and headed for Pacific Coast Highway. He easily blended in with the traffic that was always there, no matter what time of night or day.

Mon Dieu. That was close. Someone must have seen us and called the cops.

Pierre passed a police car going in the opposite direction at a high rate of speed, its siren blaring and the light bar on its roof flashing red.

Stay calm. The police can't hear the bass drum sound of my heart beating. Just a few more miles and I'll be home, assuming I don't have a heart attack while I'm driving. I hope to hell the kid got out of there all right. Fortunately, he doesn't know who I am. I paid him cash and our only contact was through the Internet. There's no way he could ID me. Have to admire him for planning on staying and continuing to work at the gallery. He's right, though. If he left, the cops would be pretty sure the robbery was an inside job and he'd be arrested. This way, with no evidence, he should be fine.

Pierre continued north on PCH, entering the 55 freeway at the far end of Newport Beach as he made his way to the 405 freeway north to Long Beach. He consciously dropped his shoulders as the tension from the robbery and near run-in with the police began to leave.

I'm getting too old for this shit. I wish there was some other way, but the economy being what it is, Darya's business is down and she can't help as much as she has in the past. I hate stealing and being nothing more than a common criminal, but I've got to do it for the little girls. Actually, right now all I want is a glass of scotch on the rocks and a good cigar. I deserve it after tonight.

CHAPTER 21

Pierre pulled his car into the apartment parking garage, relieved he hadn't seen any more police cars. He looked around, but at this time of night the garage was quiet. The only thing he could hear was the hum of the overhead fluorescent lights. He put his key in the trunk lock, opened it and carefully slung the bag over his shoulder. He'd been in such a hurry; he didn't even know which artists' paintings he'd stolen.

His large white Manx cat jumped down from his normal spot on the bookshelf as Pierre let himself into his apartment. "Good boy, Chat," he said, smiling to himself at the name he'd given the intelligent cat. Chat simply means "cat" in French. Guests at his home always thought it was a wonderful French name for a cat. He never told them he was calling the cat, "cat." It was his own private little joke.

Pierre checked to make sure that the blinds were drawn in the apartment, and then he poured himself three fingers of Johnny Walker Black Label over ice, his personal favorite. He walked into his office and took the hand-carved humidor out of the bottom drawer of his desk. Opening it, he spent a moment simply inhaling the aroma of the cigars he'd bought from a wealthy Cuban who regularly dined at his restaurant. He selected one and carefully lit it, smiling as he savored the smell of the contraband cigar. Walking back into the living room, he turned on all the lights and began taking the paintings out of the mesh bag.

Mon Dieu! I had no idea that the gallery had paintings of this caliber. I saw their ad in the paper and went in there a couple of times, but I don't remember these. They should sell well in Provence.

He leaned the paintings against the wall, took a long sip of his scotch and spent several minutes looking at them. They were all landscapes by California Impressionist painters from the early part of the 20th century. Even though he couldn't afford expensive paintings like these, he greatly appreciated fine art and read everything he could about the subject. He knew there was quite a market for paintings of this type in the United States, but he also knew too many questions would be asked if he tried to sell them here.

He was certain he could sell them in the Provence region of France. Most of the galleries in the small villages there featured landscapes, not all that different from these. Now it was just a matter of getting them there. He began by removing them from their frames. It would make transporting them much easier.

Darya had told him they'd be traveling to Marseille late next week. He hoped she'd paid the immigration and customs people enough so he wouldn't have any trouble getting them into the country.

He finished the cigar and scotch, put Chat under his arm and headed for bed. He and Darya were flying to San Francisco tomorrow morning and he needed some sleep.

CHAPTER 22

For the third time in the past hour, Pierre opened one eye and stared at the orange numbers on the digital clock on the nightstand next to his bed. The numbers on the clock read 3:30. He groaned and wished he could will himself to sleep, but his mind was spinning with the all of the thoughts that prevented him from falling asleep. Through the open window, he could hear the sounds of the night filter into his bedroom - a car alarm, a barking dog, and lawn sprinklers rotating.

Well, it's no use. I'll be lucky to get any sleep. Since Darya's cause is the reason I got to bed so late, maybe I should just tell her I can't make it to San Francisco.

He thought back to when it had all began, his first meeting with Darya in June of 2006. He'd worked in five star restaurants up and down the West Coast. One would be hot for a year or so, only to be surpassed by another one. He was a top quality chef and a rarity in the restaurant world – a chef who didn't want a restaurant of his own. That made him very, very employable. Having a top-notch chef who didn't dream of one day opening his own restaurant made owners and chef-owners very comfortable. He literally had his pick of these restaurants. The years of rigorous training at the Cordon Bleu and then learning every aspect of the kitchen brigade, that famous and rigorous French restaurant system, had paid off.

Just thinking about Darya brought a smile to his face. She was the most formidable woman he'd ever met. He recalled that night nearly four years ago when Slade Kelly, a longtime friend and well-known private detective, had made reservations for five people for dinner at his restaurant.

The maître d' knew that Slade and Pierre were friends and had gone to the kitchen with a VIP alert. Slade had given Antoine a note for Pierre with strict instructions on how Darya's food was to be prepared and when it was ready, he wanted Pierre to personally bring it to her. Pierre was no stranger to odd requests, but he'd never been asked to personally take the food he'd prepared to a customer.

When the salads were ready, he followed the waiter to the table, knowing that everyone in the restaurant was looking at him. They couldn't believe he was personally taking a salad to a customer. As was customary, the name of the restaurant was on his sleeve which partially covered the tattoo of a French chef's knife displayed on his upper arm. He wore a toque, the unbrimmed hat the head chef of a restaurant was expected to wear.

Bemused, he remembered the evening well and how furious he had been. Slade had requested that he taste Darya's salad and entrée to make sure it hadn't been poisoned. Over the years strange food requests had been made to Pierre, but none that strange. Looking back, he realized Slade had done it for a purpose.

An hour after he'd performed the taste test, Antoine handed him a note. It was from Darya.

Chef Yount, the meal that you prepared was the best that I have ever eaten. I'm sorry Slade asked you to be my taster, but in my country it is not so strange. I am well aware that I have many enemies who would like to see me dead. The men with Slade are my bodyguards. They are never far from me.

I would like to meet with you tomorrow. Please come to the address below at 10:00 a.m. I have a proposition for you, one I think you will be very interested in. See you then.

He'd quickly jotted a note to her telling her that he was busy tomorrow and gave it to a passing waiter who was going into the dining room. The waiter returned a few minutes later with the note. "Sorry Chef, but everyone at that table has left."

Swell. Now what? Merde, I guess I might as well go see what she has to say.

CHAPTER 23

The address Darya had given Pierre was a large cosmetic manufacturing firm. He pulled into the parking lot the next morning and walked into the tastefully decorated reception area. Brightly colored Afghan rugs hung on the walls in various patterns and colors and were scattered on the floor. It was a feast for the eyes.

Pierre walked up to the reception desk, gave his name to the beautiful dark-haired sloe-eyed woman with a perfect olive-skinned complexion, and told her that he had an appointment with Darya Rahimi.

"She's on a long distance conference call, but I think she'll be through in a few minutes. I'll tell her administrative assistant you're here. Please, have a seat. May I get you some coffee or tea?"

"No, thank you, but I was wondering if you might tell me what Ms. Rahimi's position is with the company."

"You don't know?" she asked incredulously. "She's the owner of the company. She started it a number of years go. She exports her cosmetics all over the world. She's a very important woman in the international business community."

The receptionist was clearly taken aback that Pierre had an appointment with a woman who was the owner of the company and he didn't even know who she was.

In a few minutes a woman wearing a black burkha came into the reception area. "*Monsieur* Yount?"

"Yes."

"Please follow me. I am Mahsa, Ms. Rahimi's administrative assistant. Ms. Rahimi is ready to see you." He stood up and followed her to the rear of the building and up a curved staircase. There was a large reception area and a desk in the center of the room with the name and title of the administrative assistant prominently displayed on a desk plaque.

On one side of the door leading to her office a nondescript looking man looked him up and down and gave him a hard stare. He looked slightly familiar and then Pierre remembered seeing him at the dinner the night before. He presumed he was Ms. Rahimi's bodyguard.

The young woman knocked on the door.

"Mahsa, please show *Monsieur* Yount in, then you may leave."

"Welcome, *Monsieur*," Darya said, coming from behind her desk to shake his hand. "I'm glad you were able to keep the appointment I requested. Please have a seat."

"Knew you'd be here," a voice said to his left. There, seated at the conference table, was Slade. "Welcome to Miss R's world."

Darya had jet-black hair swept up in an elaborate chignon. There was just the slightest hint of color on her flawless

136

olive complexion. Her large brown eyes were accentuated by a sweep of smoky eye shadow and mascara. She wore large black diamond earrings and a ring with a large lapis lazuli stone surrounded by pavé diamonds. The design of the ring was repeated in the bracelet she wore. The simple yet expensive jewelry from Afghanistan was set off by the pale blue suit she wore over a cream-colored camisole. Multicolored Jimmy Choo peek-a-boo shoes indicated that although she might be a very successful businesswomen, she was no stranger to the latest fashions.

"You see that I'm not wearing the burkha as Mahsa does. Even though I'm originally from Afghanistan, I have found that when I wear a burkha it tends to dominate business conversations and people focus on it rather than what I am saying. I only wear it when I am in Muslim countries.

"But that's not why I asked you to come today. I travel constantly and I don't like to go through what happened last night. Slade feels that I am a target of Muslim extremists and my life could be in danger. Women from my country are not supposed to be successful or own their own business. There is also the problem of a book I wrote that was critical of the ritual of female sexual mutilation that is common in Muslim countries. To say that it was not well received in those countries would be the understatement of the year."

"Excuse me, Miss Rahimi, I've never heard of that."

She walked over to a bookcase and pulled a book from it. "Here. This is my book. Read it and you'll see why I don't have much of a fan base in Muslim countries."

She went on. "I was lucky. My parents came to this country when I was sixteen and I was educated here. I started my company and it has proved to be very, very successful. The reason I've asked you to meet with me today is that I would like to offer you a job as my personal chef. It would mean that you would cook all my meals – we have a professional kitchen here in the building. When I'm traveling, you would travel with me. My plane has a well-equipped kitchen. In addition to me, you would cook for my pilot and whoever is traveling with me, usually my secretary and my bodyguard, Lou. I have two others who relieve Lou. One of them is always with me. Even when I sleep, they are near and trust me, they are very loyal, very protective, and very dangerous."

"Thank you very much, but I am very happy where I am now. I'm honored that you would like me to work for you, but I must say no."

She continued as if he hadn't spoken, "I know that you are a well-known chef and earn a very nice income. I am offering you the salary you are getting now plus an additional $50,000 annually. When you travel with me you will have your own accommodations, paid by me. Wherever I go I use limousine services. In other words, all expenses will be paid. It's a nice way to see the world. All I ask is that the food be of the caliber it was last night and of course it goes without saying that no one else touches or prepares my meals but you."

A thought suddenly occurred to Pierre. "Ms. Rahimi, do you go to France often?"

"Yes, I have a manufacturing plant near Marseille. Why do you ask?"

"I grew up in the small village of Travaillan in Provence. My elderly parents are still there. I try to travel there at least once a year, but it's expensive and it's often difficult to get that much time off. How often do you visit your plant there?"

"I usually go every six weeks or so for a few days. At least every two months."

"My father was a hunting guide until he had a very bad accident. He had to quit hunting. In fact, it's hard for him to even walk. My mother is going blind. I am an only child, so you can imagine how I feel when I leave them, not knowing if it's the last time I'll ever see them. For these reasons as well as others, I have reconsidered your generous offer and yes, I would like to accept it. When do you want me to start?"

"When can you?"

"I want to give at least two weeks' notice to my current employer. There are two very talented sous-chefs in the kitchen. Either one of them would do fine as the head chef. I will give notice this evening. Thank you and I look forward to being your personal chef. Please give me a list of foods that you like and don't like. I want to prepare the kinds of meals you're used to and that you like."

"Chef Yount, welcome to my company. I liked you when I met you last night and considering how much time we'll be spending together, that's a very important consideration. Slade speaks very highly of you and I've learned to trust him. Please call me when you find out exactly when you can start. I will make sure that we go to Marseille as soon as you begin."

Darya stood up and shook Pierre's hand. She opened the door and introduced him to the bodyguard sitting outside the door to her office.

This may be the most bizarre thing that's ever happened to me. I can't believe I took a job with a woman I just met and that I'll be seeing my parents on a regular basis and I'll be getting a pay raise of $50,000. This is turning out to be a very good day.

PROVENCE, FRANCE JUNE, 2007

CHAPTER 24

After landing in Marseille, Darya, Lou and Pierre had been able to get two hours of sleep before the limousine driver came to pick them up and take them to Travaillan to see Pierre's parents.

Lou sat next to Darya. She'd told him she didn't need him to come, but he was adamant. He said Slade would fire him on the spot if he ever found out that she had gone off on her own without him or one of the other bodyguards traveling with her.

"Pierre, when did you leave France?" Darya asked as the limo made its way north along Route 7.

"About twenty-five years ago, when I was nineteen, I went to the Cordon Bleu and graduated at the top of my class. I interned in France, actually we call it staging. Anyway, I was fortunate to be allowed to stage at several of the best restaurants in France. I worked my way up and was the sous-chef at several of them and eventually was hired by a very wealthy group of investors to be the head chef at a prestigious restaurant they were opening in Paris. I stayed there for five years. I never married and had no ties in France other than my parents. I'd always wanted to go to the United States, actually, who doesn't? When the opportunity came, I jumped at it.

"But what about your parents? Weren't they getting older by then?"

"Yes, but they were in good health. Papa was a well-known hunting guide and worked almost every day. I think it kept him healthy. Maman was busy watching over the pigs, the sheep and the chickens. Then Papa had a bad hunting accident and never could guide again. By then I had formed a new life in San Francisco. I had friends, a wonderful job, and I loved the United States," he said. He was clearly agitated, making little circles with his thumb on his pants. "It was very hard for me to stay in the United States. I decided to send them as much money as I could and visit them often. That is exactly what I have been doing."

"Do you ever regret your decision?" Darya asked, looking him straight in the eye.

"No. If I had stayed here I wouldn't be able to spend much time with them and I don't think they would have understood it. Chefs work late hours and sleep in the early part of the day and then return to the restaurant almost as soon as they wake up. I still have some friends here, but not many. I don't regret my decision, but I question it every time I visit them. It is very hard."

She put her hand on his. "I can see that it is. Why don't we stop and get some groceries for your parents when we get to Travaillan?"

He smiled, the pain visibly lifting. "That would be very nice. They never complain, but going to the market is getting harder and harder for them. Maman has a friend who drives her once a week, but my mother is going blind, so it is not easy. Papa is in so much pain that it is out of the question for him to drive. Thank you. There is a very nice market not too far up the road."

In a few minutes he gave the driver directions and as they pulled into the parking lot they were conscious of being the center of attention. Not many limousines were seen in this small rural village.

They got a shopping cart and Pierre began putting groceries in it, things that required little preparation. It was overflowing as they made their way to the check stand. Darya went ahead of him and handed the cashier her Visa card.

"Miss R, thank you, but I can pay for these groceries. You don't need to do this."

"I know I don't need to do it, but I want to."

"Well, if you insist, but again, thank you."

They loaded the groceries in the trunk as Pierre gave the driver instructions on how to get to his parents' home. After a few moments, Pierre said, "*Ici, ici,*" to the driver who stopped the car in front of an old farmhouse. Darya and Lou stared in amazement at the rusted junk, chickens, and weeds in the area surrounding a dilapidated old house which was clearly in need of numerous repairs.

Pierre told the driver and Lou to get the grocery bags out of the trunk and take them around to the back of the house. As they made their way towards the house, Pierre held Darya's arm so she wouldn't trip because of the cracks in the sidewalk. The wooden steps leading up to the house were canted at an awkward angle and the porch sagged. A blue framed door surrounded glass that was thick with dust and cobwebs. He knocked on the

door and opened it while Darya stood in the background.
"Maman, Papa, *bon jour*!"

Darya could see an old man and woman standing just
inside the door. Pierre hugged the woman and kissed her on each
check, "Ahh, Maman, it so good to see you."

He turned to the old man and put his hand on his
shoulder. "Papa, you look well. I am so glad I could come even
though it's just for a little while. We brought you some
groceries. Let me open the back door so the driver can bring
them in."

The old man looked out at the gravel road and saw the
limousine. When Pierre returned his father said, "What is that?
Why don't you have a taxi or a rental car like you usually do
when you come to visit us? And I see a woman. Have you
brought a special woman that you want us to meet?"

Pierre laughed inwardly. *No, Papa. Why do you think
I'm living in West Hollywood?* "No, this is my employer.
Remember I told you I travel with her and cook for her. We'll
only be in France for a few hours and she uses a limousine when
she travels. She has a big staff and it's easier than trying to
arrange for a lot of taxis." He motioned for Darya to join him.
"Maman, Papa, I want you to meet *Mademoiselle* Rahimi. She is
my employer."

"Welcome to our home," *Madame* Yount said. "Any
friend of Pierre's is a friend of ours. Please, come in and be
seated," she said as she led them into the living room.

As Darya looked around the old house, she knew why Pierre had wanted to go to the United States. Everywhere she looked, there were signs of neglect. It was as if the soul of the house had died and nothing new had taken its place.

"Thank you. Whenever we come to Marseilles, Pierre is quick to leave and come here. I am glad that he is able to do this. It is a silly thing, I know, but the limousine saves me time. If you would like, I could have my driver take us for a little drive. I would like to see some of the countryside. Would that be of interest to you?"

"*Oui,*" the Younts said in chorus, thinking who they could tell about this wonderful experience they were about to undergo. Darya helped *Madame* Yount to the limo and was followed by Pierre and his father. Lou and the driver held the doors open for them. When they were seated, Pierre gave instructions to the driver while Lou took a seat in front with the driver

It was a part of France Darya had never seen. Although she'd visited Paris and Marseilles many times, the rural experience was completely new to her. She was awestruck at the beautiful acres and acres of lavender, grape vines and sunflowers. The bright Provence sun made the colors jump off of the land. It was glorious. After traveling nearly ten miles, they turned around and made their way back to the Younts' home. As they approached the Younts' home, Darya noticed a large barn several yards behind the house.

"Do you keep horses?" she asked.

"*Non*, Mademoiselle," Pierre's father said. "When I was hunting I always had two, but we had to sell them after my accident. I could not take care of them. The barn is vacant now. Someday Pierre will have to decide what to do with this property. I don't think he wants to come back here and live."

"Papa, don't talk like that. I know you and Maman have health problems, but you're a long way from leaving this property. It's been in the family for generations before us. And it will probably be here for generations after us."

"But who would live here? There is only you and some of our nieces and nephews." He brightened for a moment, "Maybe one of them would want it."

"Maybe they would, but it's not something we need to worry about today. Another time," he said as the car stopped in front of the rusty gate leading to the house.

"I'll stay in the car, Pierre," Darya said. You see your parents in. *Madame, Monsieur,* I am very happy that I had this chance to spend time with you. Your son is a wonderful chef and a fine man. You should be very proud of him."

"We are, *Mademoiselle,* we are," the old rheumy-eyed man said as he shuffled off towards the front door of the house.

A few minutes later, Pierre returned and breathed a sigh of relief. "I know it's silly, but I always dread what I'm going to find when I come here. They would not trouble me for anything and I worry about their health."

"I gather from what I heard that you have some relatives here. Are they nearby?"

"Yes. They check on my parents from time to time and there are some village people they have known their whole lives who do as well. But it's my responsibility and I'm so far away. It's a burden. They are both used to working hard. That gave them a reason for living. Now they feel useless, as if they were a drain on me and everyone else. I wish there was something I could do."

And well you might, thought Darya. *And well you might.*

SOUTHERN CALIFORNIA   APRIL, 2007

CHAPTER 25

Darya and her staff flew to Paris, then on to Bangor, Maine for refueling and to clear immigration and customs as they entered the United States. During the flight, she feverishly made notes and tried to figure out how she was going to pay for all of the expenses related to the Afghan girls. Her aunt's inheritance would help in Kabul, but there would be costs for getting the girls into Marseille as well as the United States, plus additional living costs for them in both places. At some point in time, her aunt's inheritance would run out and if and when there was a downturn in the economy, it would mean cash flow problems for her business.

She tried to get some sleep, but it was fitful at best. It wasn't just the money; it was trying to figure out what to do with the girls once they got to the United States. If they were discovered by the authorities, would they be handed over to Child Protective Services, and then what, returned to Afghanistan? She had no answers and didn't know where to find them.

All she had now was a person who would allow the little girls to leave Kabul and a person who would let them in and out of France. From the way her aunt looked and spoke, she knew she didn't have much time to come up with a workable plan. She had to figure out a way to get them cared for in France, transferred to the United States, and then housed in the United States until they were adopted.

148

As the sleek jet touched down at the Santa Monica airport, Darya said, "Thanks, Mike, as usual you've made another perfect landing. It feels good to be back in the United States. I don't think I'll need you for a few days. I need to take care of some business here. Get some rest. I'll let you know when our next trip is."

The bright sun had burned off the early morning fog and as usual, traffic was a nightmare in the west part of Los Angeles. Even though she only lived a couple of miles from the airport, she knew it would take well over an hour to get home.

"Pierre, why don't you go get some sleep and then I'd like to talk to you. Let's meet tomorrow morning at ten in my office. I won't need you tonight. There's plenty of leftovers in my condo frig. Tesla, you too. Go home and get some rest. The office doesn't expect us back until tomorrow anyway. The rest of today is a bonus for all of us. See you both tomorrow." She stepped into her waiting limousine as Lou held the door open.

Darya lived in a large condominium in Malibu. When she was a young girl she'd spent many a summer at her grandparents' vacation home in Pakistan on the Arabian Sea. She loved the ocean and at an early age she'd vowed to live near it permanently. The first thing she did when her company became a success was to buy the condominium.

At the time it had been an outrageous expense, but as the years went by, it had turned out to be one of the best investments she'd ever made. Evening walks along the beach with the sand clinging to her feet and the sharp scent of salt air filling her lungs made the pressure and stress of her job worthwhile.

She took a long nap and late in the afternoon, put on a Versace T-shirt, a pair of Robert Cavelli jeans, flip-flops, Gucci sunglasses, and headed for the beach, Lou's replacement a discreet distance behind her. At the end of two hours, a plan began to form in her mind. Pierre would be an integral part of it and she was glad she'd scheduled the meeting with him. The stress of the last few days finally caught up with her. She walked up the steps to her condo, entered the glass enclosed indoor/outdoor kitchen and turned to look at the sunset. The last rays of the sun were bleeding into the ocean as the sun seemed to drop over the edge of the ocean. The sight never failed to fill her with awe.

Turning away from the sunset, she opened the refrigerator and saw the bottle of Cristal champagne she kept for special guests at the back of the refrigerator.

Looks good, but I'm too tired and it would just go to waste. Another time. Think I'll opt for the New Zealand sauvignon blanc which is already opened. That and a couple of crackers with cheese and I'm through for the night.

She mouthed good night to her bodyguard and walked down the hall to her bedroom. The next thing she knew, the shrill ring of her alarm clock thankfully woke her from a nightmare she was having about little girls trying to escape from a house of horrors. Monsters, zombies, blood, gore, and body parts surrounded them.

Drenched in sweat and with her heart beating so fast she was tempted to call 911, she made her way to the shower. A few minutes later her heart rate had returned to normal and the pulsating water from the shower had washed away the remnants of the nightmare.

This was unchartered territory for her. She was used to being in control of everything in her life and generally one step ahead of it. She was very intelligent and had formed a vast network of resources, so she was never caught off guard by shifts in public buying habits, the economy. or anything else which might affect her life or her business.

Darya's parents had brought her to the United States when she was sixteen. Even though she'd avoided the worst years of the war in Afghanistan, she was no stranger to the pain caused when loved ones were violently separated by untimely deaths. Her extended family in Afghanistan had seen its share of its members die.

She had few friends. Darya was from a culture where the females of one's family were a woman's main support group and when she left Afghanistan, she left her support group. She'd never tried to replace it with female friends in the United States. Intimate female relationships were of little interest to her.

She enjoyed men and their company on her terms, usually for very short periods and for very specific reasons. She was a woman with strong desires, but intimate relationships held no interest for her.

The only people she was really close to were her parents, but they lived on the East Coast, on the other side of the continent. Her father was a professor of history at Harvard and her mother spent most of her time drawing attention to the unfair treatment of women in Afghanistan. She saw them several times a year for a couple of days and talked to them, particularly her mother, almost daily.

In addition to being a very astute and successful businesswoman, Darya was well known to a number of people for a book she had published several years earlier on the inhumanity of the practice of female genital mutilation, entitled *"Female Genital Mutilation Victims – A Lifelong Hell."* She particularly liked the Arabic word for hell, *Jahannam*, but decided people wouldn't know what its meaning was when they read the title of her book. Although female genital mutilation was practiced by some cultures in Africa, the book was primarily aimed at Muslims.

Darya remembered the only time she heard her mother raise her voice in anger. It was directed at Darya's great-aunt who told Darya's mother that Darya would become a *"sharmuta,"* a "whore," because Darya's mother refused to allow Darya to undergo the ancient rite. It was shortly after that incident that her parents and Darya moved to the United States to begin a new life.

She'd studied at Columbia University and received a Master's Degree in Cultural Studies. Her thesis became the basis for the book. From the time it was published, she became a target of hatred by devout Muslims, particularly those living in the Middle East where the practice was common. She'd been fascinated with cosmetics since she was a little girl and decided to get a Ph.D in chemistry. She knew she'd need if it she was to fulfill her dream of having her own cosmetics company.

On one of her earlier trips to Kabul, she received a phone call about a problem at her manufacturing plant. Although it was late at night, she immediately left her hotel to see what she could do to resolve the problem. It was probably a life-saving decision. When she returned, the manager greeted her.

"*Madmozel,*" he said, wringing his hands. "I am so sorry. I don't know how these people got into your room. Thanks be to Allah you were gone."

"What are you talking about?"

"Someone broke into your room and went through everything, slashing your clothing and destroyed your personal effects. They pulled the drawers open and threw your clothes all over the room. Even your make-up and perfume bottles were poured out. The Afghan National Police are in your room now, getting fingerprints and looking for clues as to who did this horrible thing.

"The intruders, whoever they were, spray painted the walls of your room with the words 'Death To All Non-Believers.' Again, I apologize. Oh, there are the officers now. They must have finished."

She wheeled around and faced two policemen wearing the drab green uniforms of the Afghan National Police. "What have you found? Anything?"

"Nothing. No one saw them and no one heard them. Based on what they did to your room and the death threat spray painted on the wall, it looks like you have become a target of their hatred. Do you have any idea what this is about?"

Yes, but I won't be telling you. The first thing I'm going to do when I return to the United States is get a bodyguard. I am so lucky that just by chance I happened to be out of my room.

"No, I can't imagine what this is about." She turned to the manager, who was standing nearby, still wringing his hands. "I assume that I will be reimbursed for the cost of replacing everything, since this happened when I entrusted the hotel to protect my belongings."

"Of course, *Madmozel*, just tell me how much we owe you and I will have our bookkeeper give you a check before you leave."

"Thank you. I don't want to stay here tonight. It's almost dawn. Please have your concierge make a reservation for me on the first flight back to the United States. I would like you or one of these policemen to accompany me to my room to see the extent of the damage."

"*Madmozel,* a thought. Did you leave your passport in your room?"

"No. I carry it and all my valuables with me. I will be able to leave the country with no problem."

"Ahh, I am so glad. I will go to your room with you," he said, nodding to the two policemen as they left.

Darya didn't feel safe until she was back in her condominium in California. She vaguely remembered attending a business luncheon at the Beverly Hilton Hotel when a woman at her table was talking about a private detective she'd used when she suspected her husband of having an affair.

She remembered writing the private detective's name down on one of the hotel's business cards, but couldn't

154

remember what she'd done with it. She went into her office and opened the lower drawer in her desk. Darya pulled it all the way out and there, jammed against the back was the Beverly Hilton Hotel business card, and the words "Slade Kelly" written on it.

Although it was already five-fifteen in the evening, she decided to call and leave a message to have him call her first thing in the morning.

The phone was picked up after it rang once. "Slade Kelly here."

"Mr. Kelly, my name is Darya Rahimi. You don't know me, but your name was given to me several months ago. For some reason I kept the card with your name on it, never thinking I'd need a private detective, but I think I do. I'm concerned for my personal safety. When are you free to come to my home and talk to me about this situation?"

"Right now's good. Where are you?"

"I'm in Malibu, just off the Coast Highway on the ocean side."

"Gimme your address and I'll be there in a few."

Thirty minutes later there was a knock on her door. "Who is it?" she asked.

"Slade here and lady, you need a peephole in this door if you're concerned about your personal safety."

155

She opened the door and stared at the seedy looking skinny man in front of her. He wore a fedora hat that had clearly seen better days. His blue suit had shine on the elbows that told of one too many times at the cleaners and there was a cigarette dangling from his lips.

"Mr. Kelly, please come in."

"First off, Doll, the name's Slade, like in blade, you know, knife blade. Har, har, har."

What have I done? Anyone who looks like this can't be any good, can he? Well, he's here and I need some help.

She told him what had happened in Kabul and why she thought she was targeted. When she spoke about female genital mutilation, she noticed him shiver.

"You done a good thing, Doll, writin' that book. I need to know a cupla other things. You got a business?"

"Yes, I'm the owner of Darya Cosmetics. My company ships all over the world and has manufacturing plants in Marseilles, London, New York, Hong Kong and Kabul. I'll be expanding to several more cities in the near future."

"So, ya travel a lot, right? Got your own plane or fly commercial?"

"I have a company plane for domestic flights, but I fly commercial for international flights. I'm thinking of buying a larger plane."

"Anyone travel with you?"

"Occasionally my secretary goes with me. If I had a larger plane, I'd probably be able to take more people with me."

"Who hires your people and are their references checked out?"

"Well, I have a Human Relations Department that does all of our hiring. I assume they check out everyone."

"Here's what I'm gonna do. You need a bodyguard, like right now, and at all times in the future. I'm thinkin' round the clock, 24/7, here at your home, at work, and 'specially when you travel. I guarantee sumpin' like what happened in Kabul's gonna happen here. Surprised it hasn't already. Count on it. I'm gonna have one of my bodyguards come over right now. I'll get two more tomorrow. They'll work in shifts. If you got more than one with you, you get too many eyeballs lookin' atcha. Keep it low key. You got an extra bedroom in here?"

"Well, yes, but…"

"No buts. Guards gotta sleep, but they'll be wired. All you need to do is push a button and you got a gun there in two or three seconds. My guys are discreet, so if you wanna do whatever, ain't no problem."

"Thank you, but there's very little 'whatever.'"

"That's a damn shame with a body like yours. Better find some more 'whatever.' No use wastin it."

Darya could feel her face begin to turn red.

Slade continued, "Coupla things more. I want to talk to them people in HR who's doin' the hirin'. Needs some names. Also, you got a car? Drive yourself to work?"

"I'll get you the names of the HR people and yes, I drive myself to work. I have a Mercedes."

"Sell it. Put it on Craig's List or whatever. I don't want you drivin' ever again. Easiest thing in the world to fake somethin' going wrong with the car and you and the car sail over one of them cliffs on Pacific Coast Highway. From now on you're taking a limo. From what I'm hearin' and seein' you can afford to hire one. I deal with a good limo service. The bad guys can't get to their cars to plant a bomb or play around with the brakes. They're locked up and it's a lot safer for you. What about a cleanin' service here?"

"I have a housekeeper who comes in twice a week. She'll be here tomorrow. Her name's Molly."

"One last thing, Doll. Who fixes your food and where do you get it?"

"Uh, often I just order in or have some cheese and crackers or something like that."

"Oh, that's rich. Like no one could poison the food being brought in. Not real smart, Doll, not real smart. What about lunch? Somebody at the company fix it for you or do you go out to eat?"

"Both. I've never thought about this."

"Doll, from what I know of some of these extremists, you've been livin' on borrowed time. Actshully, I'm staying here until my guy gets here. I'll text him. Gotta beer?"

"No, I have a chilled Sauvignon blanc or Cristal champagne."

"Got any whiskey? Could use a cupla fingers. Been a long day."

"No. What would you like?"

"Well, damn. Ain't gonna pass this way 'gin. Might as well pop that Cristal. Ain't never had none of that."

Darya poured them both a glass of Cristal and before she could put it back in the refrigerator, Slade thrust his empty glass back in front of her. "That's good shit. Want another one, Slade? Yup, don't mind if I do. Why, thank you," he said.

As he slurped another large drink from the glass there were four knocks on the door. Slade answered it. Standing at the door was the most average looking man in the world. Brown hair cut short, medium build, T-shirt, jeans, jacket, and tennis shoes. No one would ever take him for a bodyguard.

"Lou, come in and meet your new boss, Miss Rahimi, he said, motioning Lou in. "Miss Rahimi, meet your main bodyguard, Lou."

She pulled Slade aside. "This guy sure doesn't look like a bodyguard to me. Is he really a bodyguard?" she asked.

"Yeah, in answer to your question, this man's a killing machine. He spent ten years in Asia learning the art of killing and paralyzing people. I mean Lou could put a finger on your neck and exert pressure in jus' the right place and you'd be lookin' at stars layin' on the floor. Trust me. You ain't got no more worries. Lou's here. By the way, the limo will be out in front at 8:00 tomorrow mornin'. Driver's name's Dave."

"Doll, gotta leave. See you tomorrow. Fill Lou in on the routine and show him where to sleep. Nite, kids." He handed Darya his empty glass, opened the door and walked out.

Darya simply stood by the front door for a moment, in a daze, not sure what to do next. She felt like she was losing any control she had over her life and now she was being asked to trust this stranger with her life. Her dazed condition was broken by Lou's voice.

"Miss Rahimi, if you'll show me where my room is, I'll put my suitcase in there and I'd like you to give me a tour of your condo. I'll check the exterior. Then I need to know your daily routine. Things like where you go and what you do. Will that be all right with you?"

"Yes, and I guess I should say 'Welcome to your new home.'"

CHAPTER 26

Darya woke up feeling vaguely uncomfortable. Sitting up she remembered that Lou was in the room across the hall. She saw the small black button concealed on the side of the nightstand and it all came back to her. Lou had called a contractor who worked with Slade and insisted that he come and install the device at that late hour. It consisted of a thin wire which strategically followed the top of the molding to the bedroom door, down it, under the hall carpet, and into Lou's room. It was invisible to the naked eye. While the contractor was there, Lou told him he needed to take care of some other things Lou felt were needed to improve security at the condo.

The contractor installed sensor lights on her porches and in the living room. Dead bolts were installed on all three doors, front, back and garage. A peephole was installed in the front door. After a while, Darya went to bed, leaving Lou to oversee the contractor. She was so exhausted and confused, with time changes, she wasn't even sure what day it was or when she'd last slept. The last thing she remembered was pulling the sheets down.

She glanced at her clock and realized she had about an hour until the limo driver would arrive to pick her up. Two other guards were coming to the office today to meet her. She didn't know what all this was going to cost, but figured the company could pick up the bill for protecting its president. With a strange man now living in the house and others to follow, she was very glad her bathroom was located within the bedroom suite. She wouldn't have to walk down the hall half undressed. She sighed as she realized her days of drinking coffee and reading the Los

Angeles Times at the kitchen counter in nothing more than a bra
and panties was over. She'd always loved the tinted glass on her
floor to ceiling windows. She could see out, but early morning
beachgoers couldn't see in. She decided that was probably good
for security.

Lou was standing at the front door promptly at eight and
after he checked the locks, they walked to the waiting limousine.
A man dressed in a black suit who she presumed was Dave was
standing by the open back door.

"Hi, I'm Darya Rahimi. I guess we'll be seeing a lot of
each other. This is all new to me so you'll have to tell me what to
do," she said, shaking his hand and getting into the car.

"If you let me know in advance where you want to go,
I'll check the best routes so we don't waste time. I can stay
wherever I take you until you're ready to leave or you can tell
me to come back at a certain time. It's entirely up to you."

"Well, not having done this before, it's going to take
some getting used to. As for today, I think Slade told you I was
going to my office. I'll be there all day, so there's no reason to
stay. I'll call you when I'm ready to leave. How long will it take
you to get back to my office?"

"Text me instead. I think it's more secure. If you could
give me around thirty minutes notice, that should be fine unless
there's some sort of an accident and traffic's tied up. Our secure
storage lot isn't that far from your office and I'll go back there
when you don't need me."

"That sounds fine. As I said, this is new to me, so if I can do something and make it easier for you, let me know."

Dave was an excellent driver and in just a short time the limousine pulled up in front of her office. He opened the door and she and Lou got out. She walked through the front door and greeted the receptionist.

"Gina, I want you to meet Lou. He has free rein of the company from now on, so you don't need to call me and tell me he's here. Oh, and I'm expecting a man by the name of Slade Kelly this morning. Please send him up. I know him."

She walked across the reception area and went up the curved staircase carpeted in a soft mauve color. The white walls were decorated with rugs from the Middle East. She smiled at Lou, "Hope you don't mind the climb, but with my schedule there's no time for a health club, so this is my workout."

"Fine by me, Miss Rahimi."

"Lou, that sounds too formal. We're going to be spending a lot of time together. Why don't you call me something else?"

"Okay. How about Miss R? I like that."

"I do too. And I must say your grammar is a whole lot better than your boss's."

"Miss R, don't ever underestimate Slade Kelly. His speech and the way he dresses are just part of his simple country boy cover up. Did you know he has a Master's Degree in Criminology as well as a law degree?"

Darya came to a dead stop, turned around on the stairs and looked at Lou with a wide-eyed expression on her face. "You're kidding, right? He seems like such an uncouth boor."

"Nothing could be further from the truth. He's a great believer in smoke and mirrors. You can learn a lot more when people think you're not very smart. Words slip and people get sloppy. If someone thinks you're smart, they're going to be a lot more careful about what they say and do."

They climbed the rest of the stairs in silence. Darya was having a hard time adjusting to what Lou had just told her.

"Good morning, Miss Rahimi. Welcome back. I hope your trip was successful," her longtime administrative assistant Mahsa said.

"Well, that's a long story, too long for now. I'm glad to be back, Mahsa. I want you to meet Lou. He's my bodyguard and will be…"

She was interrupted by Mahsa, "Your what?" she practically screamed, her big brown eyes opening wide in disbelief. "You're kidding, right?"

"I wish I was. There are going to be some major changes in our day-to-day operations. Lou or one of his men will be with me at all times, plus I can't drive my car anymore and I have to use a limousine service. Oh, and a man named Slade Kelly will be here in a little while. Let me know when he arrives. Call HR and find out who hires new employees. I want a report prepared, if there's not one already, describing the exact procedure we follow when hiring new employees. Let me see it before Slade gets here."

"Miss R, while you're getting that information, I'd like to look around this area, your office, and the restroom and just make sure everything is secure. Is that all right?" Lou asked.

"Of course, Lou. If you need anything, just ask Mahsa."

She opened the door to her office and as always, it brought a smile to her face. Pillows in brightly colored Middle Eastern fabrics were placed on the backs of two cream colored couches. In between them was an intricate tiled table covered with beveled glass. Floor lamps with brightly colored shades repeated the colors of the pillows.

Moth orchids in deep pinks, purples and cream were on the coffee table and the credenza set against the wall near the large conference table. The colors and fabrics definitely indicated this was a woman's office.

Darya sat down at her desk and within minutes was engrossed in her email. She spent the next hour responding to it, stopping only to look at the HR report Mahsa brought in. Just as she was finishing with her email, her intercom rang. "Miss Rihami, Slade Kelly is here. Shall I show him in?"

"No, thanks. I'll come out and get him." She stood up, walked to the door and opened it. "Good morning Slade. Come in. How are you?"

"Well, Doll, well," he said, getting up from his chair. He ignored the shocked look on Mahsa's face. She'd never heard anyone call Miss Rahimi, "Doll!"

"Slade, I had HR prepare a report on our hiring protocol. Here it is. Mahsa will take you down there and introduce you to the two people who are responsible for hiring all of the employees at Darya Cosmetics. When you're through, why don't you come back up here and we can go over it?"

"Sounds good. Lou behave himself last night?" he said with a lewd smile on his face.

"Yes. He's a very nice man. He called the contractor you work with and the two of them secured the condo last night. He's in the process of assessing what I need in the reception area, my office, my private bathroom and my secretary's office. It's all coming together."

"Good. Good. Okay, Doll, got lots going on today. Let's get this HR thing out of the way."

She pressed the intercom button. "Mahsa, Mr. Kelly's ready to go down to HR." She stood up and opened the door for him.

"I'll see you back here when you're finished. If you need anything, please call Mahsa."

Lou walked out of the bathroom. "I've completed my inspection and I don't see any problems. What I would like to do is the same thing I did last night at the condo. I want to have the contractor install a button you can use for me or my men as well as a dead bolt lock. If someone should get past the bodyguard and your administrative assistant, you can use the dead bolt to secure the room. It will give you time to call 911 and might just save your life. I'd prefer that the contractor makes changes only in your presence. Do you have any appointments this morning?"

"No. Actually, I don't have any appointments all day. I always try to keep the day after I return from a trip free because I know there are things that are going to need my immediate attention and I want to keep my concentration clear. Go ahead and get started. I hope you're not offended if I ignore you."

At noon, there was a knock on her door. "Come in," she said.

Slade opened the door and said, "Doll, I don't want you to ever say that again. No matter who is out here, even if he tells you he's the fuckin' President of the United States. From now on Mahsa's to call you on the intercom and tell you who's out here. If you don't know who's on the other side of the door, don't open it and throw the dead bolt closed. Now, let's get some lunch unless you got other plans. HR's closed for an hour and I got time. Do you want to go out and get something?"

"No. We have a lunchroom and kitchen on-site. We're too small to have a cafeteria, but a catering company delivers sandwiches and some other things. There are a couple of food machines as well. Some people bring things from home, so we have a microwave and a refrigerator. We can get something down there."

"Don't see no problem with that, do you Lou?"

"No. If the caterers are bringing in sandwiches for the group, they can't single out Miss R."

"Lou, we'll bring you back sumpin'. Whadda ya want?"

"Some kind of sandwich with meat and cheese, some chips, and a coke if they have one. If not, I'll take some water."

"Okey dokey. C'mon Doll, I'm starving. Let's get some eats and bring 'em back here."

They spread the sandwiches, chips and fruit out on the conference table in Darya's office. "Looks like the two meatheads who've been doin' the hirin' have done a piss poor job and I'm real leery 'bout a coupla guys you got working in bookkeepin'."

"What makes you say that?"

"Well, I called the references of the last ten employees the HR people had hired and none of 'em had been called before. Makin' me more nervous to find out two of the guys in the bookkeeping department are on a designated terrorist list. I got some friends in high places who gets me info like this when I call 'em. So, Doll, we got some problems. "

"Slade, I can't believe what you're telling me! What do you suggest?"

"You can't fire the two who are on the terrorist list just because they're on the list. ACLU be on you like flies on shit.

You can fire the two yahoos who ain't callin' the references. Sooo, you gots a couple of choices. You can put these terrorists in jobs where they can't pick their nose without someone seein' 'em or you can get one of our guys to act as an in-house spy. Your call. Lou, got any thoughts on this?"

"This makes me really, really nervous, Slade, for a number of reasons. We can't alert the rest of the employees and one of them could easily get past the receptionist and Mahsa and get in here. Hate to say it, but there's some reason they're at this plant and I'd be willing to bet it's not for the love of cosmetics! I think you need to do both."

Lou continued, "I think the terrorists need to be put in a place where someone oversees everything they do. I'd put both of them in an office with one of our men. Miss R can just say she was making some changes and that she'd hired a CPA to oversee the bookkeepers. I'd also put another one of our men in the manufacturing area. All companies do that from time to time and it's no big deal."

"Doll, whaddya think?" he said, stuffing chips in his mouth while he was still eating his sandwich. Darya thought she might be sick.

A master's degree? A law degree? You've got to be kidding me!

"At this point, I don't know what to think. From what you're telling me, I'm probably lucky to be alive and that the plant hasn't had a bomb placed in it. Slade, I've trusted you this far. What do you think I should do?"

169

"Don't talk about it much, but my company's a lot bigger than it looks. Yeah, I can get a guy in here that'll look like he's the cosmetic CPA king. Put those two wannabe terrorists in a room with him and that's one down. Thinkin' we need a mole in the plant. That place is big and is absolutely ripe for a bomb or sumpin'. Depends on how much they hate you. Want to tell me why? Smellin' it's more than cosmetics. You mentioned somethin' bout a book and female genital mutilation last night.

She put down her sandwich, took a deep breath and told them about her strong feelings on female genital mutilation and her book. Last night she'd mentioned it to Slade, but today she went into detail. She told them how the book had been banned in all of the Muslim countries and that her face and the cover of the book had been on television sets throughout the Muslim world.

"It was number one on The New York Times Non-Fiction Best Seller List for over a year," Darya told them. "The Christian countries were outraged that the practice still existed and the Muslim countries were outraged that anyone would doubt the sanctity of their age-old rites. It caused quite an international stir."

Lou had never heard of the practice and was clearly shocked that it existed. Slade was not. "Doll, don't tell many people this, but I gots some degrees. In one of my classes, actshully a class on feminism, had to write a paper on a ritual or practice still bein' done, but bein' challenged by modern women.

"Never forget a woman in that class. We went for some java. She was Egyptian and tol me 'bout the practice. Her mother wanted it done to my friend's daughter. Left Cairo and hadn't spoken to her mother since. Wrote on that subject. No wonder you're being targeted."

"So, Slade, the swearing, the poor English and everything else is just a facade. You're really quite a deep and intelligent man, aren't you?"

"Have my moments, Doll, have my moments. So, I gotta get a guy for the white collar side and one for the blue collar side. Right?"

"Yes. Go ahead. What shall we do about the HR people?"

"Fire 'em. And it's with cause. It's real clear that they gotta call the refs for prospective new hires and they ain't been doin' it. That's a no brainer. Have the head of HR fire 'em today. Give 'em two weeks' pay and have 'em clean their desk out at 4:00 and be gone at 5:00. I'll supervise it. Don't you worry. Slade's on the case. Oh, Doll, one more thing."

"Good grief, isn't all of this enough, Slade?"

"Not if I'm gonna keep that pretty face and them gorgeous legs of yours in one piece. You need a personal chef. Someone to cook everything you eat. He or she can make a bunch of things to keep in your condo and here. What really bites my butt is thinkin' of you eatin' in them restaurants in Kabul. Jesus, Doll. You've been lucky."

"Slade, this is going to end up costing me a fortune. People better keep on buying cosmetics," she said, laughing.

"Okay, I'll cut ya a little slack on the chef thing. By the way, went over to your condo this mornin' to meet the cleaning lady. She's okay."

"As they say in the country where I was born, 'Praise Allah.' At least there's one thing that's been good today.

"Doll, I need to make a coupla calls, get my guys over here this afternoon. Don't mind me." He furiously punched numbers into his phone and after about twenty minutes said, "Okay, Doll, got two guys comin' here at 4:30." One for the plant and one for the office. Need to figure out how to get the two terrorists relocated into the same office with my guy. Need to see whatcha got open in the plant so my other guy can fill that position. See you later."

APRIL, 2007

CHAPTER 27

"Did you get a chance to catch up on your sleep?" Darya asked Pierre. It was the morning after they'd returned from Marseille when Darya had met Pierre's parents.

"Yes, but the older I get, the harder it is. I love seeing my parents and traveling, but there is a price to be paid."

"Pierre, I have a private matter I want to discuss with you. It involves something that's completely outside the scope of your job duties as my personal chef, but it's something that's terribly important to me." She told him about her aunt and the little girls in the orphanage her aunt had founded on the outskirts of Kabul.

"Here are some photos I took. Pierre, it's a tragic situation and I know these little girls simply represent the tip of the iceberg. I can't stand by and do nothing, plus I've made what is probably as close to a deathbed promise as one gets, to try and get them to the United States and placed in loving homes. I know it won't be easy, in fact, it's very dangerous. Considering the threats…"

"What? You never told me you were being threatened. What are you talking about? Are these recent threats?"

"Recent enough that Slade is upping the security on my home and everywhere else by adding another guard. This one will be in charge of the external things like the outside of this building, my home, and the hangar where I keep the plane. A number of these threats have been delivered by mail and phone threats have been made as well."

"Well, I've told you before and I still feel this way, Slade Kelly is the best in the business and so are his people. You will be fine. He turns down about 99% of the people who apply to work for him. Character checks, background checks, demonstrations of their martial arts skills, and firearm tests are just part of what he demands. His people are fiercely loyal to him. No, you're in the best hands you could be in."

"Well, that makes me feel better, but that's not why I wanted this meeting."

He looked at the photos once again and then raised his head and spoke quietly. "I've never seen anything this horrific outside of some movie, but this is real, isn't it?"

She paused and took a drink of water, red fingernails highlighted by the clear glass. "Yes. It's very real. Pierre, I remember seeing a barn on your parents' property and I even asked them if they had horses. They said it was vacant. I have a proposition for you concerning the use of the barn. What do you think your parents would say if you asked them if we could use the barn to temporarily house the little girls while we treat their wounds and feed them some proper food?"

She sat back in the large black leather chair, hands steepled in front of her face and looked directly into Pierre's eyes. She could almost see his mind working.

"Miss R, I don't know what they would say. They watch TV, in fact, it's one of the few things they still can do, and even though the images are blurred for Maman, she can hear the voices, so they both know about the tragic situation in Afghanistan. In fact, the grandson of one of their friends was with the French Army in Afghanistan. He was killed by a roadside bomb. They don't believe France should have any military involvement in Afghanistan and were glad when most of the French troops were pulled out."

"I would pay them rent for their barn. Of course I would also pay to have the barn renovated for the girls. They'll need to have people who can stay with them while they are there. Perhaps your parents know people in the area who would like to earn some extra money by caring for the girls."

"A good friend of mine is a doctor," Pierre said. "I could call him and see if he would treat the girls for a minimal amount. I can't walk away from these pictures and do nothing. Let me call my parents and talk to them." He looked at his watch as he stood up. "It's about 7:30 p.m. there now, so it's a good time for me to call. I'll step outside."

While he was gone, Darya once again looked at the photos of the young girls. She knew that each of them had probably been subjected to female mutilation and there was nothing she could do about it now.

No, what's been done has been done, but I can do everything in my power to see that these girls are given a chance for a better life. The American dream is certainly better for them than the Afghan nightmare that's a certainty.

A few minutes later Pierre walked back into her office, a big smile on his face.

"I'm taking it that your parents agreed, am I right?"

"Yes. They agreed so quickly, it surprised me. I think they've been a little bored and are tired of dealing with their infirmities. This gives them a purpose. They said to tell you thank you and that they would make some inquiries about renovating the barn and getting some help. I'll call my doctor friend later and see if he would be willing to help us too. I told my parents that the little girls would not be in France legally, so they should be careful who they talk to."

"Oh, Pierre, this is absolutely wonderful. I'm so glad. That's one huge problem out of the way. Let me jot down some notes on what needs to be done to the barn. Actually, it's pretty minimal. I think we'll need three rooms. Probably a big room with a kitchen in it. I don't think most of them know any English and I'd like them to learn a smattering of it before they come here."

"That's a good idea, Miss R, but how do you plan to do that?"

"Well, if we can get some chairs and make the room into a kind of classroom, they could actually do a little school work and learn some English. Even if it's only a little bit, it will help them. We'll need a bathroom with one or two toilets and sinks and a room where we can install bunk beds for them to use as a dormitory. Do you know if there's a water hook-up in the barn? It sure would be nice if we didn't have to pay for that."

176

"I don't know what condition it's in, but yes, I remember a water spigot near the barn door. When I was a kid I had to fill big tins with water for the horses. Of course that was a long time ago. But Dad hunted until the last couple of years and he had two horses he used. The water must have been working then. I'll ask."

"Pierre, I'm going to want you to oversee this. I'm too high profile and questions would be raised if I talk to the contractors or the women we need to hire. However, it would make perfect sense for the Younts' son to take care of the barn renovations and other things that will need to be done. "

"Miss R. I'm happy to do it. This makes me feel good."

Darya continued, "I can dovetail a business trip to Marseille so we can oversee this project. I need to get started on this project like yesterday. I don't think my aunt has more than a couple of weeks to live, so we're really under the gun. If I have to sweeten the pot to get the work done faster, then so be it. Just get it done."

Her intercom rang. "Yes? Show him in." She put down the phone. "Slade's here."

"Hey Doll, how's it goin'? So what's so 'portant that I had to get out of bed at this ungodly hour? Had a late, late night," he said with a smirk on his face. "Coulda used a few more Z's."

177

"Sorry, Slade. Let's move over to the conference table. Sit down. I want to show you some photographs." She passed the pictures across her desk to Slade. He spent a few minutes looking at each one and then raised his eyes to her.

"What the hell is this all about?" he said in a low gravelly voice with no trace of his usual massacre of the English language.

She explained the situation to him and how Pierre's parents were going to house the girls while they were in France. "Here's where I'm at, Slade, and Pierre, this will be news to you as well."

Darya took a cluster of red grapes from the fruit bowl on the long conference table and slowly began eating them. "I've already taken care of a few things. When the girls leave Kabul, they will have no ID papers, passports or anything to verify their identity. The Kabul and Marseille Immigration Officers are willing to look the other way when I take the little girls out of Afghanistan and bring them into France and take them out. Naturally, I'll be paying them well to look the other way.

"Slade, Pierre just arranged to have his parents temporarily house the little girls in a barn behind their home in a remote village in Provence. We're working on having it renovated, finding clothing, hiring a couple of local women to care for them, and making sure we can get some medical attention for the girls."

"Wow, Doll. Ya been busy!"

DIANNE HARMAN

"My aunt is dying of cancer and time is running out for her. I'll be going back to Kabul at the end of next week to see her, probably for the last time. I want to be able to tell her that her legacy will continue. The only person who knows about what she is doing is her driver. I'm not quite sure how we're going to handle that. I'll work that out when I get there. Any questions so far?"

"No, looks like you're doin' fine. Whadda ya need me for?"

"I can't figure out how to get them into the United States. My plane doesn't have a fuel range that would allow it to fly non-stop from Marseille. When I travel to or from Europe I usually refuel at Bangor, Maine. I know they'll have to go through some type of immigration here in the United States.

"Even if I could fly non-stop, I took one look at the immigration officials at the airport I usually use here in California and knew there was no chance of anyone allowing something illegal to be overlooked, no matter how much I paid. Plus, I know Miami won't work. There was a huge scandal at the Miami airport last year and they're being extra careful. I need some ideas on how I can get these girls into the United States, and then, don't forget, once they're here, I've got to find somewhere for them to go and hopefully, have loving families care for them."

All three of them were quiet as different ideas passed through their minds and just as quickly were rejected. "Doll, I got an idea. Gonna need your plane. Pierre, can you cook a bunch of stuff this afternoon for Miss R to eat during the next couple of days?"

179

"Sure, what do you have in mind?"

"I need you to come with me to the Cayman Islands. We'll have the plane take us, spend a day or two, pendin' on what happens and then come back." He turned to face Darya, "Call your pilot and tell him I want to leave tomorrow. Just be Pierre and me and the pilot."

"I got rid of Mike's co-pilot when you told me I was to be his co-pilot. You said the fewer people who knew where I was, the better. Mike will need a co-pilot for the flights. I don't want problems with the FAA. Just a moment."

She called Mahsa. "Call Mike and tell him I want to talk to him. I'm not sure where he is. I told him to take some time off, but I need him. You have his cell phone number. Thanks."

"Assuming you can solve that problem, Slade, I've got one final problem I need help with. What am I going to do with these little girls when they get here? I can't keep them at my condo."

"Doll, think I can cover that problem for you too. Had some dealings with a Reverend a few years ago. He had a big church in the valley. He's gone now, compliments of yours truly, but I 'member they did something with 'doptions. Let me check and get back to you. Reverend kinda hated me, but since he's gone now maybe I can talk them folks at the church into helpin' out. On second thought, don't think I better get 'rectly involved in this. Pierre, why don't you do this cuz no one knows you. I'll get the information to you. At some point you're gonna need some type of ID for these kids. I can get passports for them."

The intercom buzzed on her desk. "Yes, Mahsa, I'll take it." She picked up the phone on the conference table. "Good morning Mike, I'm sorry to bother you but something has come up and I need you to fly to the Cayman Islands for a day or two. Pierre and a man by the name of Slade Kelly will be flying with you. It will be just the three of you, plus you'll need to hire a co-pilot.

"I'll have Mahsa make reservations at a hotel for you and arrange for a limo service to shuttle you from the airport to the hotel. Let her know what time you'll be landing. Why don't you take off around nine in the morning? That'll get you in just before dark. Thanks and again, I'm sorry for the short notice. By the way, I'm going to want to go back to Kabul the latter part of next week."

She buzzed Mahsa again and told her about the trip to the Cayman Islands. "Work out the times with Mike and then arrange for four rooms at a nice beach hotel. Let Slade and Pierre know the details."

She looked at her watch and saw that it was 11:30. "I'm going to have to wind this up. I have a lunch conference here in my office. Pierre, why don't you bring the food up around 12:30? I'll talk to both of you later. And I know I don't need to tell you that this conversation was private and what has been said is to stay in this room."

"Not a problem, Doll," Slade said getting up from his chair. "The Cayman Islands. Woohoo! Can't wait to see them hotties on Seven Mile Beach. Ain't been there in a while. Talk at you later."

COYOTE IN PROVENCE

What a character, but what would I do without him. Is there anything he can't do?

CAYMAN ISLANDS   APRIL, 2007

CHAPTER 28

Mike landed the big Gulfsream G550 with ease at the Owen Roberts airport on Grand Cayman Island. He taxied to the International Terminal as Slade and Pierre retrieved their carry-on luggage and prepared to go through immigration.

"Nice job, Cap'n Mike. See ya at the hotel. I'll call you and tell you when I wanna leave. Have some fun while you're here, but just watch out for them little umbrella drinks. They can be a bitch the next mornin'."

Thirty minutes later Pierre and Slade walked to the waiting limousine. The airport was only four miles from the hotel, just enough time for them to feel the island's warmth and see the sparkling Caribbean Sea. They checked in and got their room keys.

"Need to make a coupla calls. Meetcha in the main bar in 'bout half an hour," Slade said.

Pierre swiped his card key in the lock and the green light blinked. He opened the door and stood there for a moment, drinking in the view. The Caribbean was calm and the sun was close to sinking over the horizon, with blue, mauve and orange colors blending into one another. The sky and the horizon were a bright crimson red with their colors changing every moment as the sun sank over the horizon. It was magnificent.

Wow. What a sight. I wish I could paint this, but I don't think there's an artist alive or dead who could do justice to this scene.

He walked into the room, set his suitcase down and decided to take a quick shower. Ten minutes later, refreshed, he left his room, glancing out the window at the ocean's horizon, which had changed into the robin's egg blue color of early evening.

The bar was doing a very good business. Vacationers, businessmen, and a couple of women who looked like high priced hookers crowded the room. He ordered a vodka tonic, taking to heart Slade's words about umbrella drinks. He'd had a few mornings like Slade had described and he wanted to be careful about his drinking as he wasn't sure what tomorrow would bring, or even the rest of tonight. He figured he'd find out when Slade arrived.

He didn't have long to wait. Just as the bartender brought him his drink, Slade walked in. He sat down at a table and gestured for Pierre to join him. He got off the barstool and joined Slade. "Well, any luck with your phone calls?"

"Yeah, let me get a drink. I could use a couple, but we gotta take it easy, might have a long night ahead of us." He gestured to the waitress and ordered a beer. "Here's the deal. We got a meetin' at 8:00 tonight in a seedy little beach bar down the road. Woulda gone to Kaibo Beach, but it's too far to walk and I don't want anyone payin' attention to what we're doin'. Limousine don't xactly say 'not doing nothin',' particularly at some sleazy bar. Think they know 'xactly what we're doin'."

"And so just exactly what are we going to be doing?"

"Hirin' drug runners."

"What?" Pierre said, as he choked on his drink. "I'm not getting involved in drug running. Why in the hell would we do that?"

"Don't get your shorts in an uproar. Ain't runnin' drugs. Just hirin' drug runners. Big difference. See, here's the thing. Few years ago one of my clients had some things he needed to get out of the Caymans and get into the U.S. We knew there was gonna be problems, so I found some drug runners who took him into a lil' airport in North Carolina. These guys fly low, under the radar. Paid 'em a lot of money and knew they'd 'member me. And they did."

"I still don't see what drug runners and planes have to do with us."

"Those little girls gotta get to the U.S. Miami's out. Can't bribe nobody there. People at this little shithole North Carolina airport are on the take, big time. We'll fly the girls from Marseille to here in the Caymans, then you and one of my men will fly with the girls in two planes to the North Carolina airport where Mike and the Gulfstream will be waitin'. Once they go thru U.S. Immigration there, they're home free. Can fly into any airport 'round LA and just sashay off the plane. No sweat."

"Okay, I have a question. If this airport is so small, why does it have a U.S. Immigration office?"

"Tobacco, my friend, tobacco. Need bodies to work the fields and when it's time to harvest, that damn airport is up to its eyeballs in banana and coconut island people. Gotta have someone makin' sure they can get in the U.S .- legally," he said winking.

"But where's the drug connection? I hear you talking about tobacco, but what about the drugs? And these planes? Who owns them?"

"Ya don't wanna know. Runners fly in there with drugs that are offloaded to waitin' cars. Plane lands and people are paid off. Immigration and customs are both on the take. I mean, what the hell? Who's gonna know in that small airport? Been doing' it a long time."

And no one's ever been caught?"

"Nope. Just kind of sumpin' everyone knows 'bout, but the pays right, and even the dear City Fathers are gettin' their share. Them elections are the most highly contested elections in the U.S. Some yahoo had them 'dopt term limits, so every eight years it's a feedin' frenzy in town. Anyway, we're meeting Arsene later. Let's get somethin' to eat."

"Wait a minute. What if we're followed? And who does Arsene work for?"

"Why would we be? Just a coupla guys having a drink with one of the locals. Probly think we'd like to get us a coupla coconut honeys. Don't worry, security's my job. I don' know who Arsene works for and I don' wanna know. He's just Arsene

– the man who can get them little girls to the land of milk and honey."

"It's show time," Slade said after they'd finished eating. He signed the credit card bill the waitress gave him. "Here you go honey. Might be back a little later. Wait for me. It'll be worth it."

Pierre and Slade walked through the lobby and took the steps leading to the beach. It was a beautiful night. When they opened the glass door, they were greeted with the smell of the tropics, suntan lotion, salt air and a whisper of island flowers. Well-lit yachts formed a skyline against the dark blue of the Caribbean.

"How far is it?" Pierre asked. "If we're going to walk in the sand, I think I'll take off my shoes."

"Don't wanna ever take your shoes off in coconut land. Never know when you're gonna have to run. The Caymans are lookin' good for the tourists, but you scratch the underbelly and the maggots come out. Keep 'em on. It ain't too far. 'Bout a coupla city blocks. Actually, looks like Roberto's palapa up ahead."

In the distance Pierre could see twinkling lights covering a small thatched roof hut. As they got closer, he could make out the word Roberto's etched on a wooden plank attached to a stick in the ground with an arrow pointing to it.

Roberto's was just a round open-air bar in the sand with a thatched roof covering it. Candles on the bar provided the light.

It was a perfect place to meet someone when you didn't want to be seen.

Slade walked up to a dark-haired man sitting at the bar. Everything about him said he was a local, from the color of his deeply burnished skin to the surf shorts and flip-flops he wore. He turned around on the bar stool and smiled at Slade. "Nice to see you, Mon. Grab a beer and we'll go sit down on the chairs on the beach and look at all the yachts."

"Arsene, I want you to meet my friend Pierre. Pierre, this is Arsene." The two men shook hands. They got their beers from the bartender and followed Arsene.

"Join me," Arsene said as he sat down in a beach chair. Roberto's was a little too seedy for the upscale tourists who frequented Seven Mile Beach, but the locals loved it, and Roberto made sure he didn't miss a drink sale because there was no room at the bar. Near the shoreline, beach chairs had been haphazardly arranged.

"Okay, my friends. You're the ones who wanted to see me. What do you need?"

Slade had taken notice of every person in the bar and the two women sitting in beach chairs a few yards from them. He didn't see anything that set off the alarm bells that were always on alert in his head.

"You and some of your people helped me out a few years ago. Got a little problem that's going to be ongoing. Need to get about fifteen or so little girls outta France from time to time and into the U.S. Pierre, here, will have their passports so

188

they can get into the U.S. They're from an orphanage in Afghanistan. Here, take a look at these pics," he said, handing the graphic pictures of the mutilated little girls to Arsene. "Here's a flashlight so you can see 'em better."

Arsene was quiet as he leafed through the photos. It was impossible to look at the pictures of the little girls without wanting to help them. "Okay, Slade. What do you have in mind?"

"I know you got some contacts with people who have planes. Thinkin' we could bring the girls here and then you could fly them to that little airport in North Carolina where your people got immigration and customs on the take. Know those planes aren't big enuf for all of 'em, so thinking we'll need two planes. Pierre can go with one group and my other man with the second group, say maybe ten minutes or so apart. Got someone with a big plane that will meet 'em at the North Carolina airport and take 'em to California," he said, finishing off his beer and putting the empty bottle in the sand as he lit a cigarette. "Whaddya think?"

"It's going to cost you. It'll be $10,000 each plane, each time, half down and the other half when we land, plus $2,500 each plane for immigration."

"Sweet Jesus, Arsene, you're twisting my balls."

He shrugged. "You want to get those girls into the U.S or not? Your choice, Mon. That's the deal."

"How safe is it?"

"Never have had a problem. Immigration rarely checks on that airport. Everyone knows illegals are probably coming in to work the tobacco crops, but the owners almost singlehandedly elect the politicians, so everyone's real quiet about what goes on there. The word's out to leave it be. Kind of nice for us. Allows for a little drug action as well. So, what do you want to do? I've got another meeting in a little while. You're not the only one who needs something."

"Ain't got no choice, do I? Yeah, we'll take it. How much notice you gonna need?"

"One week will be fine. You have my number," he said, standing up. "Nice to meet you, Pierre. Good seeing you again, Slade. Always nice to do business with a repeat customer. I'll wait for your call." He looked at his watch and hurried off.

Slade dropped his cigarette into his empty beer bottle. "Bingo. Good to go," he said as he started walking back to their hotel, Pierre following.

"Slade, you left your bottle in the sand."

"Yeah, let some local kid get the cash back on it. He can use it more than Roberto can. You okay with leavin' tomorrow? I'll call Mike and tell him. Need to get back and get some place for them little girls to stay once we get 'em to California."

DIANNE HARMAN

SOUTHERN CALIFORNIA   APRIL, 2007

CHAPTER 29

Pierre, Slade and Darya sat at the conference table in her office the day after the two men returned from the Cayman Islands. Pierre filled her in on what had taken place.

"Nice job, gentlemen. I think everything's in place with the exception of what we're going to do with them when they get here. Slade, you talked about a church you thought might be interested. Have you done anything further with them?"

"Doll, they'd like to see me hangin' from the highest tree. Just say I had a little somepin' to do with their beloved Reverend havin' to leave rather sudden-like. Pierre, like I tol' you before, you're gonna have to do this one. I'll give you 'structions,' on what to do."

"Slade, I don't know a damn thing about kids or adoptions. Are you sure I'm the right person for this?"

"Yeah. You're a natural. Here's the deal. I've written down the name of the church. It's evangelical and they don't cotton much to Muslims. Know it ain't politically correct to say, but it's the truth. Call 'em and make an appointment with the minister. Tell 'im there's some little orphan girls who are bein' smuggled out of Afghanistan and show him the pictures. Tell him they need homes to stay in until they're 'dopted. Tell him there's a humanitarian group that's doin' this, but you can't give him their name."

191

"Everyone else has their hand out. Will he?"

"Don't think so. 'Member, this is a church. Think they'd be doin' it for God and for some of their members who are having a hard time 'doptin. If he talks about money, tell him they could get some from the 'doptive families. Actshully, they could probably make this into a little business for the church. Total difference from human trafficking. These little 'uns will be goin' to lovin' homes, not sold into some type of sexual slavery. Got any questions?"

"No. I just hope it works."

"Well, better get to know this guy cuz you'll be the one deliverin' little girls to him in the future as well."

"Okay. I might as well get started. Let me have that paper and I'll see what I can do." As he left the room, he pulled his phone out of his pocket and placed the call.

A few minutes later he returned with a big grin. "I've got an appointment this afternoon. If we can put this last piece of the puzzle in place, we'll be good to go."

Pierre continued, "Miss R, I was on the phone with the contractor in France before I got here this morning and since there's already running water in the barn, he thinks it's just a matter of putting up some interior walls and installing a bathroom. He doesn't think it will take more than two weeks. He's already started. Plus, I hired two women who are old family friends. They're retired and bored. The thought of a little extra money helped. They're getting some clothes and bedding. When

DIANNE HARMAN

you first told me about it, I never thought this thing would work, but now I think it's going to."

"Great. Please call me after your meeting and keep me up to date with what's happing at your parents. Slade, anything else?"

"Not for now. Got a little honey I got to check out for hubby. He's pretty sure the pool guy is hosin' his wife. One of my men's over there now, scopin' it out. Pierre, call me," he said as he left.

Pierre took a deep breath and sat back in his chair as he said, "Well, Miss R. This has been a good couple of days. You're doing a very good thing and each one of those little girls owes you her life."

"Thank you, Pierre, but they owe my aunt their life. Next week when we're in Kabul we'll need to figure out how the orphanage can go on when she's gone. By the way, I'm almost out of food at the house and also here at the office, so please make some meals for me. Oh, and I'm having a dinner party at the house tomorrow night. Some big investors. Would you do something spectacular, like maybe marinated leg of lamb with all the trimmings? They kind of expect lamb, me being from a Muslim country."

"No problem. I'll make a meal for them they'll never forget and they can just open up their checkbooks. How does that sound?"

"Perfect," she said, smiling.

193

PART THREE

PROVENCE, FRANCE   SEPTEMBER, 2010

CHAPTER 30

Jordan and Elena left Avignon and drove the short distance to Orange, and then on to Travaillan. Chef Bernard's directions were excellent. Within minutes they were looking at a very small rundown little house with a dilapidated barn barely visible behind it.

"Do you hear children's voices?" Elena asked as they got out of the car and picked up the two sacks of food. "I swear I hear kids, but I can't imagine where the sound is coming from."

Just as Chef Bernard had said, there were several rusted appliances in the yard and chickens roamed freely. Faded tattered clothing gently swayed on a clothesline. Litter and trash were scattered everywhere.

"Elena, be careful and watch where you step. There may be some broken glass." They gingerly made their way to the glass-paned blue front door which was badly in need of a fresh coat of paint. The glass was too grimy to see through it. Everything cried out to be repaired or cleaned. Jordan knocked on the door.

While they waited for his knock to be answered, Elena looked around. The dilapidated house and the neglected yard reminded Elena of her childhood home where her family still

DIANNE HARMAN

lived. She shuddered, glad to have escaped the barrio and its terrible memories.

A minute or so later, an old man opened the door. Rheumy eyes looked out at them above a body that was so badly misshapen it was hard to imagine it could move on its own. *Monsieur* Yount wore a black beret and a vest over a heavily patched shirt and dirty black pants. His belt was cracked in so many places, it was impossible to tell whether it had originally been black, brown or white.

"*Monsieur* Yount, I am Jordan Kramer and this is *Mademoiselle* Johnson. We have just come from seeing your friend, Chef Bernard, who asked that we bring you these sacks of food. He said he would be coming to visit you soon." Jordan spoke in a respectful, neutral tone.

"We're here to talk to you about your son, Pierre. He told *Mademoiselle* Johnson that he would help her find a job in a restaurant in California, but he didn't give her his contact information. Do you know how she could get in touch with him? Would you have an address or a telephone number for him?"

The rheumy brown eyes looked out at the two of them for what seemed a very long time. After he'd fully assessed them, he said, "Please, come in. I am Giles. It would be rude of me to leave you outside."

As soon as they entered the small house, Jordan spotted the Franz Bischoff painting hanging over the couch. It was a jewel and shone against the sooty old walls of the house.

So, six of the seven have been located. And who would ever think one would be in this little dilapidated house? My God,

195

that painting is probably worth $15,000 and to think it's hanging in this run-down place. The painting is probably worth more than the house and the land together. Amazing!

Giles Yount lowered himself into a chair with a great deal of difficulty, his cane by his side. "Please, have a seat. You may have to clear a space. My wife is going blind and can't see to clean like she used to. With my injuries, I'm no help to her."

"Yes, I see that you're in a great deal of pain. I'm sorry. Is there something we can get you or do for you?" Elena asked.

"No, but thank you. When Pierre comes, he cleans for us, but it has been several months since he was here. He's such a good boy. I don't know what we would do without him. He brought us that painting I saw you look at. He said we could get a good price for it, but I like it. Not many things bring me pleasure anymore, but that painting does."

"It's truly beautiful, *Monsieur*," Jordan said. "I can see why you would want to keep it."

Holding shakily on the cane as if it was an extension of his hand, he pointed it at Jordan. "I can't help you. We never know when Pierre's going to call or visit. I know he is a private chef, but I don't remember the name of the woman he works for."

They heard the sound of a car pulling up in front of the cottage, and a car door opening. "Ahh," said the old man, in a hacking cough reflecting a lifetime of cigarette use. "It must be my wife, Catherine. *Monsieur*, would you be so kind as to help her bring in the groceries?"

Jordan was out the door in a second. "*Madame*, I am Jordan Kramer, a friend of Chef Bernard. Please, let me help you with those groceries. Why don't you hold on to my arm while we go up the walk?"

He took the groceries from her and nodded to the elderly lady who had driven *Madame* Yount to town. She waved goodbye to *Madame* Yount and said, "See you next week."

When they got to the end of the sidewalk, Elena held the door open for them. Once again she thought she heard children's voices drifting through the early afternoon air.

She smiled warmly. "*Madame* Yount, I am Elena Johnson. We came to find out how I can get in touch with Pierre. I met him at a restaurant where I work. Please sit down. Here, let me help you. Jordan, take the groceries into the kitchen and I'll put them away."

Elena followed Jordan into the tiny kitchen and began to take the food out of the sacks. Everywhere she looked there was grease and dirt. She didn't want to offend the Younts by offering to clean the kitchen, so she turned on the water to get it as hot as possible while she put the groceries away. When the water was finally hot, she quickly scrubbed the sink and counters. As she was putting food in the refrigerator she noticed that some of the food in it was spoiled. She put it in one of the grocery bags and looking out the window, saw a large empty trash barrel several yards from the kitchen back door.

Walking towards the trash barrel, she was certain she heard children's voices. There was no mistaking it. After she put the trash in the barrel, she followed the direction of the sounds, which became louder the closer she got to the old dilapidated

197

barn. She took a few more steps to the barn door, opened it, and stood frozen in amazement at the sight before her.

There were fifteen or so young girls in the barn. Some had been badly burned; others were missing a limb or an eye, and a few bore huge black and blue marks, suggesting they had been beaten. They were all emaciated, many with open sores. One of the girls spotted Elena and cried out, pointing at her. An older woman quickly came to the door where Elena was standing, and at the same time, hushed the girls.

From the doorway Elena could see that the barn was divided into three rooms. The large front room served as a kitchen, and by the looks of the placement of chairs, it also seemed to serve as a classroom. Through an open door, Elena could see a room in the rear portion of the barn with bunk beds pushed up against the walls. Another door next to the bedroom opened, and a young girl came out. Looking over the girl's shoulder, Elena saw stalls and sinks in what appeared to be a bathroom. It was very stark.

"*Mademoiselle*, why are you here?"

Elena was speechless. All the young girls seemed to have been badly abused or injured, in one way or another. Two of them appeared to have only one eye. She was having a hard time taking in the sight of the injured girls in front of her and at the same time trying to comprehend how and why they were in a dilapidated barn in Provence. It made no sense.

"*Mademoiselle*, I must ask again. Why are you here?"

Elena found her voice and responded, "I came here to visit *Monsieur* and *Madame* Yount, and to find out if they knew how I could contact their son, Pierre."

At the mention of Pierre's name, the Frenchwoman seemed to relax and smiled broadly. "Ahh, yes, what a wonderful man. I don't know what we would do without him. Please, come in." She closed the barn door behind her.

"Who are these young girls?" Elena asked with a sweeping motion of her arm.

"They are from Afghanistan, part of the nearly two million orphans in that country. As you can see, all of them have suffered greatly. They had no one to turn to and were found on the streets of Kabul by a friend of Pierre's employer."

Elena turned to her, interrupting. "How were they brought here? And what will you do with them? Do the French authorities know about them?"

"*Non, mademoiselle.* Pierre works for an Afghan woman who lives in the United States and helps girls such as these. Pierre has a friend who is a doctor. He comes once a week to tend to their needs as best he can. After they have healed somewhat, and been fed nourishing food, friends take the girls to the airport, and Pierre's employer flies them to the United States."

Elena stood in shocked silence as the Frenchwoman continued. What she was hearing and seeing was unfathomable to her.

"We help these abused young girls because there is no one else to care for them. Without us, they would either be dead or forced to work as sex slaves in the brothels of Kabul. What we are doing is illegal. You can see why we must be very careful that no one finds out about them."

Elena felt like she was going to become ill. *Please don't let me be sick.* She quickly swallowed several times, willing the clammy feeling to go away. *I've never seen human beings who have suffered like these young girls. I thought the gang rape that happened to me was the worst thing in the world, but clearly these little girls have suffered far more than I have.*

"Do many people know about this?"

"No. You look like a good person. I trust you not to tell anyone. Pierre and the lady he works for arrange for clothes and food. There are a few other women besides myself who come here daily to take care of them. As you can see, the Younts are too old and suffer too much physically to be of much help in caring for them. Pierre sends as much money as he can. I think he has friends who are chefs that help, because sometimes we get sacks of food dropped off at the front door, and often there are envelopes containing money in the sacks."

She continued, "Because of what the Younts are doing, these young girls have a chance of finding homes where they will be well cared for. So far, nearly two hundred young girls in the last three years have been placed in homes in the United States." She paused and then emphatically stated, "Pierre, his parents, and his employer are saints. I beg of you not to tell anyone."

Elena had a hard time thinking of Pierre as a saint. This was a direct contrast to everything Jordan had found out about Pierre and his accomplice.

"Thank you for telling me. I didn't expect any of this when I came here. I must get back to the house. I'm sure they are wondering what happened to me, but yes, you can trust me. I will not reveal your secret to the authorities. *Bon jour, Madame.*"

As Elena walked back to the house, tears begin to form in her eyes. She could only imagine what the young girls had witnessed and the horrors they had gone through. She knew the sight of the mangled, tortured bodies she had just seen would stay with her forever. She also felt angrier than she had ever been in her life.

Elena unsteadily entered the house through the back door, walked through the kitchen, and into the living room. Jordan took one look at her and knew something had happened while she'd been outside. He couldn't imagine why she was looking and acting so strange. Although she was ashen and visibly trembling, two spots of anger were quite visible on her cheeks and her eyes were blazing. They hadn't been together very long and this was a side of her he hadn't seen.

"While I finish putting away the last of the groceries, may I start a little dinner for you before we leave?" she stuttered, as she walked over to *Madame* Yount.

"No, thank you," *Madame* Yount said. "We have worked out a system. Giles sits at the table and tells me what to put in each pan. He is my eyes and I am his body. It works for us. It's not what we would have chosen, but with Pierre's help, we get along."

"Well, it's time for us to leave. We have several other stops to make. Your husband told me you don't have any way to contact Pierre. I would like to leave my contact information with you, if I may. If you need anything, please call me. Will you promise me you will do that?" Elena said.

"Oh, we don't need anything, but yes, leave us your number and the next time Pierre calls, I will tell him you came to our house looking for him. He may call you and help you get a job with that restaurant," Giles said.

Elena took a pen and a piece of paper out of her purse, and wrote her telephone number and address on it. She also took out ten one hundred euro notes, and put them underneath the piece of paper. She knew the proud couple would not accept money if she offered it, but if they discovered it after she left, it would be too late to return it to her.

Jordan stood up. "We'll let ourselves out. Thank you so much for your time and hospitality. *Bon jour.*"

CHAPTER 31

As soon as they got in the car, Elena began to sob, flinging her head back against the seat headrest. "Oh Jordan, you can't arrest Pierre! He's all they have. Stealing the paintings from the gallery in Laguna Beach was wrong, but maybe there's a higher law working here. Please, please don't arrest him. Can't you do something to stop this investigation?"

"Let me think about it. Believe me, I don't feel any better about this than you do."

"No, you don't understand," she said between gulping sobs. "Yes, the Younts are very sad, but they're saints. Let me tell you what I saw in the barn." She paused, as the memory of what she had seen came flooding back to her.

She tried to talk again. "Remember, when we got out of the car, I told you I thought I heard children's voices? Well, when I was in the kitchen beginning to put away the groceries, I walked out to the trash barrel and again I thought I heard children's voices. I followed the sound to the barn and opened the door and, and..."

Elena was crying so hard that Jordan had no choice but to pull the car over on the shoulder of the highway. He turned off the engine and faced her, putting his arms around her.

"It was awful. They were maimed and scarred. Oh Jordan, you don't know what I saw. These poor little girls, you can't believe what they've been through and, and..." She stopped, her voice trailing off, hiccupping as she tried to get control of herself.

"Elena, you're right. I don't know what you saw. Tell me everything. Start at the beginning. I have no idea why you feel so strongly about stopping the investigation, other than how hard it was to see the Younts." He handed her his handkerchief. She dabbed her eyes with it, swallowed and began.

"Well, when I went outside to dump some garbage in the trash barrel, I was certain I heard little girls' voices coming from the barn. I walked over to it and opened the door slightly. There were about fifteen little girls inside. Some looked to be as young as a year and a half or so, probably not any younger, because they were all walking. The oldest was about seven."

"You're kidding! The children's voices were coming from the Younts' barn?"

"Yes, just listen to me. Something was horribly wrong with each of them. Oh Jordan, some had their eyes gouged out, limbs were gone, they were bruised, scarred, and some of them even had what looked like cigarette burn marks on their faces and bodies. Oh God! It was the worst thing I've ever seen." Elena sat perfectly still, with tears streaming down her cheeks, and her face ashen.

"What in the hell were they doing in the barn, for God's sake?" He took his arms away from her and looked into her tearful eyes.

"The Younts and some volunteers take them in. The mysterious person that we were told Pierre works for, well, it's a woman who lives in the United States who still has family members in Afghanistan. Evidently she takes her private plane there several times a year, and smuggles young girls out of Afghanistan and flies them to Marseilles.

"For God's sake, Elena, this sounds like it's out of some thriller novel."

"Jordan, just listen to me," she sniffled. "They live in the Younts' barn and are cared for by some local women. After they've healed somewhat and gotten a little stronger with good food and some health care, this Afghan woman that Pierre works for flies them to the United States in her private jet. I don't know the details. Oh Jordan, it was the saddest thing I've ever seen. You can't arrest Pierre. You've got to stop the investigation. If you don't, and if it continues, what's going to happen to those little girls?"

She was out of breath from trying to tell him what she had seen and sobbing so hard, her body started shaking. "Pierre and his employer are responsible for saving those girls' lives. So what if he stole from a gallery and the insurance company paid the gallery? If something happens to Pierre, there won't be anywhere for those girls to go. Jordan, you can't turn Pierre in, even if you find him."

Jordan started the car and pulled back onto the highway. "I don't know what I can do. What Pierre has done is not only wrong, it's a felony. We both know that. Does the fact that he did it for an admirable cause make it all right? I can't say. Let me think about it. This goes against everything I've ever known in my life and yet…"

205

CHAPTER 32

It was now late afternoon and they both were quiet on the drive to Aix as they thought about what had happened earlier in the day at the Younts. When they arrived in Aix, the town was bustling.

"I'd like to start by walking to the four galleries I looked up and see if it looks like any of them has the last painting, the William Wendt. There are also a couple of restaurants I'm interested in, but first I'd like to finish the search for the seventh and final missing painting," Jordan said.

They parked the car, and, as in almost all of the villages and towns Jordan had visited, the galleries were near one another, usually in the older part of town. They spotted two on the same street, slowly ambled by them, and looked in their windows to no avail. A third gallery two streets over produced the same result. Just as they were walking up to the last gallery, the proprietor turned the sign on the door from "*Ouvert*" to "*Fermé.*"

"Come on, Elena, let's go across the street and wait until the guy leaves. I couldn't see what was in the shop or even in the window, and I'd like to finish up. I don't want to have to return."

They walked across the street and when the lights in the shop changed from bright overhead lights to a dim night light, they re-crossed the street. There, hanging on the wall just inside the entry, but clearly visible from the street, was the last of the stolen paintings, the William Wendt.

206

"My God, there it is. Look at it! It's fantastic. I can't believe it hasn't sold. Although the green hills in it are a little sharper than the hills of Provence, the lavender and yellow-orange colors sure are reminiscent of the sunflower and lavender covered hills here in Provence."

"I see what you mean," Elena exclaimed. "I think I remember you telling me that Wendt was one of the leading artists of the California Impressionist movement. Looking at this painting, I can sure see why. It's beautiful."

Jordan turned to her. "I know I should be happy to find this last one, but all I can think about is what a hollow victory it is. I can't get the picture of the Younts out of my mind. If I go ahead with this, there's a good chance I'll find Pierre and he'll eventually go to prison. And then what will happen to his parents and the Afghan girls? Who's going to take care of them?

"In some ways I wish we'd never gone to Travaillan. I honestly don't know what to do. I know you want me to walk away, but this goes against everything I've sworn to do my whole life, uphold the law. Please, Elena, give me some time. Believe me, I need it." They turned away from the gallery, each with a heavy heart.

Elena was having trouble seeing Jordan's side of the dilemma. It seemed very cut and dried to her. Let Pierre go and let the little girls have a chance at living the rest of their lives in loving and caring environments. She knew she'd probably never see Jordan again after their time together in Provence, but she also knew deep inside, that if he decided to pursue Pierre, she wouldn't want to see him again.

COYOTE IN PROVENCE

As they turned to walk away from the gallery, Jordan looked at her and said, "I read a very good review in the New York Times about a restaurant in Aix called Chez Feraud. It's in the old part of the city; actually it's pretty near where we are right now, so we can walk to it. Since the French usually dine much later in the evening, maybe we can get in without a reservation."

"Jordan, I'm exhausted. I really could use some good food and wine. In some ways, this has been one of the worst days of my life. I can't take much more."

They walked the short two blocks to the restaurant and were immediately impressed with what they saw. A courtyard with a fountain, olive trees, a trellis and the requisite Provence blue shutters welcomed them into the small restaurant on the tiny street in old Aix.

Chez Feraud did not disappoint. A good Rhône wine with a dinner of pistou soup, grilled lamb, and warm figs with cold caramel ice cream for dessert lightened their mood considerably.

Jordan was just as tired as Elena, but even he was surprised at the words that came out of his mouth as they sat sipping their after-dinner coffee. He looked directly at her and said, "I think I'm falling in love with you. I've got to be honest. I didn't plan on this happening, or even expect it. Falling in love was the farthest thing from my mind. I'll admit that getting you into bed was the nearest thing in my mind, but something has gone either terribly wrong or terribly right. I know I'm not perfect. I've been told that at times I'm impatient and overbearing, and I know I've been a sexist in the past, but when I'm with you I feel different. You bring out the best in me. I don't want to be without you." He stopped talking and took a sip of his coffee.

Elena sat very still, waiting for him to continue and wondering where this conversation was going.

Jordan continued, "I'd like you to come to the United States for a visit. You can stay in my home. It's very large, and it's right on the beach in a small town south of Los Angeles called Sunset Beach. Come for a month. Let's see what happens. If it doesn't work out, you can always return to your cottage here in Provence." He stopped talking, putting his coffee cup back on its saucer. "Why are you shaking your head?"

"I can't go back to the United States," she said softly as tears began to trickle down her cheeks for the second time that day. "I left in a hurry because of memories, and I don't want to revisit them. They're too painful. You'll always be welcome at my home here in Provence. I've fallen in love with you as well, but there are things about me you don't know. I'd rather keep it like that. There is some sort of magic that exists between us. I can sense it and I know you can too. If you knew the truth about me, the magic would be gone, and you would no longer love me. Please, just let it be as it is now."

"I don't understand any of this, and I guess I'm not supposed to," Jordan said angrily, sitting back in his chair and tossing his napkin on the table. "I can't imagine there's anything about you that would cause me not to love you. Please, stop crying. We won't talk about this anymore. I was planning on doing all kinds of work tomorrow regarding this case, but I need a break. Let's go to Arles and St. Remy."

Elena nodded, tears still trickling down her face.

"I've always wanted to see where Van Gogh spent time both before and after he cut off his ear. I know it's kind of weird, but it's always fascinated me."

She looked at him, laughing through her tears.

"And as long as we'll be in Arles, let's go to the Camargue and get some of the salt the region's famous for. I don't think it's a very fair trade. You'll stay here and the salt will come to California with me, but I guess it'll have to do for now," he said smiling, dissolving the tension between them.

"I'd love to do that," Elena said. "And while we're in the Camargue, we have to go to Les Saints Maries de la Mer. That's where the Black Madonna is supposed to have come ashore. We can spend the day just roaming around, being lovers discovering Provence. I'd like to forget everything about Pierre, the paintings, the Afghan girls, and the fact that you'll be leaving in two more days."

As she spoke, her face darkened. For a brief moment she thought about the lonely days that loomed ahead for her once Jordan returned to California. She shook her head as if to ward off the unpleasant thoughts.

They left Aix and drove the short distance back to her cottage. It was a full moon and they could make out the olive groves and vineyards in the soft moonlight. Soon they saw the twinkling lights of St. Victor. They wound their way around the village, driving the short distance up the hill to Elena's cottage. It had been an emotional day for both of them, and although they were exhausted, sleep did not come easily.

Jordan kept running Elena's earlier conversation through his mind, wondering what could be so terrible that it would prevent her from wanting to be with him. He thought he knew how she felt about him, and he still couldn't believe he'd actually asked a woman to live with him. That was a first. And then to be turned down! Did that mean the only way he'd ever see her again was if he came back to Provence? His thoughts continued to tumble and turn until he finally fell asleep.

I've been so afraid something like this might happen. I wonder if I did the right thing. Yes, Elena thought, as she too, tossed and turned, *it was the right decision. We'll have two more days to enjoy each other, and then we'll go our separate ways. There's nothing else I can do.*

CHAPTER 33

Wrapped in Jordan's arms, Elena eyes flew open, positive she heard something walking on the gravel driveway in front of the cottage. Her mouth went dry, and she could feel her heart banging in her chest, certain the sound of it would wake Jordan up. She listened intently and knew she wasn't imagining it. The fields around her cottage were rife with all sorts of animals, but this sound was unusual.

"Jordan," she whispered in a raspy voice, "Wake up. I think there's someone outside the cottage. I heard something making a sound on the gravel, and I don't think it's an animal."

Before she even had the words out of her mouth, he'd silently pulled on his running pants, flip-flops, and had his gun in his hand. "Don't move," he whispered in her ear. "Stay right where you are."

He cocked his head, listening intently. He, too, heard the sound of something moving on the gravel, and to Jordan it sounded like footsteps. From the distance of the sound, Jordan knew he could get to the door before the intruder tried to enter the cottage. He slipped past the bedroom doorjamb and quietly made his way along the wall to the window. Although the shutters were closed, with the help of the full moon and a small crack in the shutters, he could just make out the form of a man standing outside the front door. It looked like he was holding a crowbar. The man was inches from the front door when Jordan yanked it open, took two steps out the door, and held his gun to the man's head.

"What are you doing here? What do you want?" he said loudly.

The man tried to answer and began stuttering. "N-n-n-nothing," he said.

"Tell me what you're doing here. If you don't tell me by the time I count to ten, I'll pull the trigger. Do you understand me? What are you doing here? One, two, three, four..."

The man was shaking so badly he dropped the crowbar on the ground. "Please, *Monsieur*, lower the gun and I will tell you what you want to know. I have never in my life done anything like this. Please, don't shoot me," he begged.

Jordan lowered the gun and repeated, "What are you doing here?"

"Pierre Yount is my friend. He called me tonight after he talked to his parents. They told him that two Americans, a *Mademoiselle* Johnson and a *Monsieur* Kramer, visited them this afternoon and asked how they could get in touch with Pierre. His parents said *Mademoiselle* Johnson told them Pierre had offered to help her get a job with a restaurant in California, and that she worked at Henri's Bakery in St. Victor la Coste.

"He remembered her, but knew he had never told her he would help her get a job. *Monsieur* Yount told him *Monsieur* Kramer liked the painting that Pierre had brought them on his last trip. When he heard that, Pierre became concerned. It is valuable and he was afraid that the couple might try to steal it from his parents. *Mademoiselle* Johnson gave his parents her address. Pierre asked me to come to her cottage and see what I could find out. I am here because he is an old friend."

Jordan looked at him. There was nothing about this bumbling older man that indicated he'd ever done anything like this before. Jordan knew if he was a professional, he would have chosen shoes that didn't make sounds on gravel, he wouldn't be wearing denim jeans that made sounds whenever he took a step, and he would have had some kind of weapon other than a the crowbar. A professional would have been much better prepared.

"Do you have Pierre's phone number?" he asked.

"*Oui.* He wanted me to call him after I came here."

"Call him. When he answers, give me the phone. I speak very good French, so don't try anything but giving me the phone as soon as you've placed the call."

"Elena," Jordan said in a loud voice. "Come out here. I want you to hear this conversation with Pierre."

In seconds, Elena was out the door and standing by his side.

With shaking hands, the intruder pressed numbers on his cell phone. When a voice on the other end answered, Jordan told the intruder to put his phone on speaker and hand it over to him. He took several steps away from the intruder, keeping his gun pointed at him, and motioned for Elena to step back as well.

Jordan spoke into the phone, "*Monsieur* Yount, my name is Detective Jordan Kramer. I am a policeman with the Art Theft Division of the Los Angeles Police Department. I know about the theft of the paintings from the gallery in Laguna Beach. I also know that you have sold some of those paintings to galleries in the Provence area and did it to help the Afghan girls

214

your parents are harboring in their barn. I even know about your employer, the Afghan woman responsible for illegally taking the children from Afghanistan to France, and then on to the United States."

Pierre replied in a strained voice, "My father told me that *Mademoiselle* Johnson had gone into the barn and seen the young girls. He knows nothing about the paintings I have sold. He doesn't even know that the one in his house is stolen or that it's quite valuable."

"I want you to make a solemn promise you will never have anyone come to *Mademoiselle* Johnson's cottage again or try in any way to contact her. If I find out that you have violated your promise, I will hunt you down to the ends of the earth, and I won't rest until you are sent to prison. Your parents will die an agonizing death because they'll receive no financial help from you, and there will be no place for the girls to go. I still haven't decided what to do about all of this, but I do know that whatever my decision is, *Mademoiselle* Johnson is not to be contacted by you, in the near future, or ever. Do you understand me?"

There was a long silence on the line, and then Pierre began to speak, "How did you find out about the paintings? I really thought they would go unnoticed in the out-of-the-way galleries I sold them to."

"Pierre, the discovery of the paintings was a fluke. Clients of mine happened to see the Alfred Mitchell painting when they were vacationing in Provence."

"I see. And yes, I promise that I won't contact *Mademoiselle* Johnson in the future. My parents said you

215

brought food to them and left them some money. For that I thank you. But how did you…"

Pierre became silent. He seemed to be holding his breath.

Jordan said, pacing back and forth. "I have several questions to ask you. In exchange, I may not turn your parents in to the authorities. I want them fully and truthfully answered. Don't lie to me. Do you understand?"

"Yes," Pierre whispered.

"Did you have an accomplice at the gallery? How did you get the paintings past customs? Who else is working with you here in France? Why is your employer doing this for these children?"

"Money eases the way for many things," Pierre replied. "It eased the way at the gallery. The young art student who worked there was very happy to have the chance to make, what for him, was a large amount of money for simply cutting a hole in the glass door after gallery hours, opening it, and disabling the alarm system. That allowed me to enter the gallery, put the paintings in a mesh bag, and leave with no trace that I'd ever been there."

So it was a type of inside job. The investigating officer's instinct had been right, Jordan thought to himself.

"As to your other questions, again, money eases the way for many things. My employer gives a lot of money to immigration authorities, both in Afghanistan and France.

Bringing the paintings into France was easy and helped to pay for the children's expenses.

"She lands her private jet at a small airport in Marseille and the children and I are met by friends of my parents who take us to my parents' home. She's visited my parents, and is just happy to have a safe place where the children can stay. French Immigration and Customs authorities at the small executive airport in Marseille where she lands have been paid handsomely to ignore the children on the plane, so when I went through customs with the paintings in my bag, I wasn't even searched or questioned. It was actually quite easy. Yes, money talks in any language."

"Go on. Tell me about your accomplice here." He covered the phone with his hand and whispered to Elena, "Can you hear what he's saying?"

She nodded, indicating that she could hear what was being said.

"You're probably looking at him," Pierre said. "He's an old friend of mine, a chef. We used to work together and have stayed in touch all these years. He knows my family well. I was afraid that the gallery owners might start talking to one another. My father was a famous hunting guide in the area, and my family and I are well-known. I've had my chef's knife tattoo for many years, long before it was popular. Many people remember it. My friend was happy to help because the money would go to help my parents and the little girls."

"Pierre, every time a case comes across my desk that involves an art gallery theft, I'm going to wonder if the items went out of the country, and if you're the one who committed the crime. I'm not going to ask you about other crimes you may have committed. From what you've told me and from what I've seen, I don't believe you or your friend did this for personal gain. Goodbye for now. I'll get your telephone number from your friend and I'll call you when I've made a decision about what to do with you."

He ended the call and walked over to where the intruder was standing, visibly trembling. "Here's your phone. I'm letting you go under one condition. You must never come back here. As you know, I spoke to Pierre, and he will probably tell you the same thing. Neither you nor Pierre is to ever come anywhere near this cottage again. Am I making myself clear?"

"*Oui, Monsieur.* I will never come back. May I go now?"

"Yes, but first I want you to write down both yours and Pierre's telephone numbers and your name. I know that you were the one who helped Pierre sell the paintings, but I'm not going to do anything about that right now. Did you come by car?"

"*Oui.* It is parked just outside the village. Thank you for not calling the police." He turned and quickly walked down the lane.

Jordan walked over to where Elena was waiting for him. "It's okay, sweetheart. You won't be bothered again. Let's go inside," he said, holding out his hand to her. She clasped it so hard he had to bite his lip to keep from crying out.

As they walked inside, she stopped and looked at him. "You know, Jordan, I think you'd like Pierre if you met him. Who knows? If things had been different, maybe you could have met at a restaurant and shared a meal."

CHAPTER 34

Jordan woke up to the smell of coffee and sizzling bacon. He pulled on a T-shirt and shorts and walked into the small kitchen where Elena was squeezing orange juice. Freshly picked flowers were in a large glass vase on the end of the kitchen counter.

What's not to like about this? He thought.

He walked up behind her, put his arms around her waist, and nuzzled her neck. "Good morning, beautiful! What's for breakfast besides you?" He undid the sash on her robe and let it drop to the floor. "My God, you're incredible. Turn the burner off; you can always reheat the bacon." He picked her up and carried her into the bedroom.

As he set her on the bed, Elena said, "Jordan, I'll say it now, but I promise no more. The last few days have been the best of my life. I want you to stay here with me forever, but I know that's impossible. I told you I can't go back to California. I just hope that on your next vacation you'll return to Provence and more importantly, to me. Jordan, I can't concentrate when you do that. No, don't stop. Oh, yes, Jordan, oh God, yes!"

Later, they lay wrapped in each other's arms. Today was to be their special day, a day to spend however they wanted.

"Stay here. I'll call you when breakfast is on the table." Elena walked back into the kitchen and retrieved her robe from the floor. The bacon was only partially cooked. She turned the burner back on while she mixed the eggs, getting ham, cheese and scallions from the refrigerator for the omelets. She sliced fresh bread and began to toast it, putting butter and apricot jam on the table.

"Jord…" she started to call out, but he was already in the kitchen, drawn by the smell of bacon. Just the sight of him filled her with conflicting emotions; happy being with him, and sad thinking about him leaving the day after tomorrow.

"Elena, this is fantastic. Maybe you should have taken a job at some high-end restaurant in Paris. This may be the best breakfast I've ever had."

"Don't think so. As I recall, you told me you loved the chocolate croissants, and I don't have any. I was going to make them this morning, but it seems someone had other plans for me. Not that I'm complaining. Far be it from me to complain about the last hour. Seriously, you're a wonderful lover. How about I cook, you make love? Will that work for you?" she said laughing.

Soon they were on their way to St. Remy. They spent the morning exploring the old 12th century monastery which had been turned into the Saint-Paul Asylum.

"Elena, look at the view from this window. It's exactly like the fields Van Gogh painted when he convalesced here. Can you imagine what it must look like in the summer when the sunflowers and lavender are in full bloom?"

She glanced idly at the brochure she'd picked up from the display rack at the tourist center. "This village is charming. It's got to be an art lover's paradise."

"Sweetheart, wherever and whenever I'm with you it's like being in paradise."

"Oh brother. I think I liked you better when you weren't so full of bullshit, but then again, it's kind of nice to hear. Thanks!"

"Don't move. I want to take your picture. I want to capture this moment forever. When I get back to California, I'll have this photo of you. In fact, I think I'll make it into the wallpaper background on my phone." He snapped a photo of her with his phone.

"I wish you hadn't done that. I'd rather be in your memories than displayed on your phone. My hair's a mess and I really wasn't expecting you to do that."

He looked at his phone and grinned. "Sorry, you're on here for posterity! And I might add that you look beautiful." It was a poignant moment, both of them aware there might never be another moment when they would be together thinking of nothing more important than a photograph on a cell phone.

Shortly before noon they left for Arles, only ten minutes away. It was the city where Van Gogh also painted and eventually died. Tourists were always at the Roman ruins and the open air market, which was just beginning to close. They wandered through the market which had everything from fresh produce to antique furniture. Vibrant colors, smells and sounds assaulted their senses.

"Elena, I want to eat at the L'Atelier de Lean-Luc Rebanel, if it's okay with you. It's a Michelin rated restaurant noted for featuring local food of the seasons."

A few minutes later they were seated at a table at the restaurant. "What looks good to you?" Jordan said. "We had a large breakfast. Want to split a salad?"

"That sounds great. I noticed when I was looking at your Michelin book it's known for its bistro salad. It has several kinds of greens and bacon mixed with a light dressing, and topped with a poached egg. That's what I think we should have. You can choose the rest. No. Wait a minute. Did you see the raspberry tart on the menu? Let's have that for dessert and some bread and wine. I guess you're not going to be able to choose the rest. I just did!"

They were quiet as they simply enjoyed the meal and each other.

"I hope you liked that as much as I did," Jordan said. "There's got to be a master chef at work in the kitchen. That was fabulous, but now I need to move around."

They walked off their lunch, visiting the ruins and going in and out of shops before leaving the city. Arles was the gateway to the Camargue, an area of salt plains, shallow lagoons, rice paddies and bright pink flamingos. They drove south to the commune of Les Sainte Maries de la Mer on the Mediterranean Sea. At the entrance to the Notre Dame de la Mer Church, they were panhandled by a number of gypsies. Elena reminded Jordan that their patron saint, Sarah, the Black Madonna, had a crypt in the nave of the church.

"What's the story of the Black Madonna?" Jordan asked, trying to adjust to the darkness inside the church. "I've never heard of her."

"Well, according to this brochure, she was the black assistant who accompanied Mary Magdalene, Mary Salome, and Mary Jacobe to France when they fled the Holy Land after the crucifixion. Supposedly, they were in a small boat and she's said to have helped them land safely. That's probably why there are so many gypsies here. I wonder if the legend is true, and if there really was a Black Madonna," Elena said.

"Who knows?" Jordan said, "But what a story!"

"Can you imagine what this must be like in May when thousands of gypsies come here on a pilgrimage to honor her? According to the tourist information I read," Elena said, "they arrive up to a week before the scheduled church ceremony to socialize, arrange marriages, and celebrate baptisms. I'd love to be here and see it!"

"Come on, Elena, I want to walk down to the beach and see if I can get a sense of the large procession the city expects when they have the blessing of the sea next month."

Like every other tourist area, even though it was small, the commune had its fair share of T-shirts, postcards, and other mementos for sale. Jordan couldn't stop himself from buying two jars of the Camargue salt.

"I know it's touristy," he said, "but I've always heard it's the best salt in the world, and the gourmet shops in the United States charge a king's ransom for it. Did you know there are gourmet food shops that have special tastings of salt and even olive oil?"

"Thanks anyway," Elena said, "but I think I'll stick to winetasting. I don't think my palate is sophisticated enough to differentiate between various kinds of olive oil or salt."

Neither one of them voiced it, but they were both grateful for the intrusion of the Camargue and the Black Madonna. It would have been too painful to spend the day talking of never seeing each other again.

As the day drew to a close, they drove back to Elena's cottage, tired from the day and ready for a good night's sleep.

CHAPTER 35

The following morning as Elena was making breakfast, Jordan said, "Elena, I need to talk to the Younts again. I'm see-sawing about what to do with the investigation of Pierre. I really need to talk to his parents and get some closure on this thing. Are you up for it? I know this is your last day of being off work and you may want to just rest, but if you could, I'd really like you to go with me."

"Actually, I've been thinking about them non-stop and wondering how I can help them. Yes, I'd very much like to go with you."

They were both quiet on the drive to Travaillan, each lost in their own thoughts. "Jordan, do you think we should tell them we know about the girls in the barn?"

"Yes. Think about it. The French woman who talked to you probably told them that you discovered the girls as soon as we left. Plus, I'd bet Pierre called his parents after I spoke with him and may have even told them I'm a detective. We need to reassure them that their secret is safe with us. They're probably concerned we'll go to the authorities."

"I hadn't thought of that. You're right."

"I couldn't sleep last night. I just kept thinking about how they're helping those unfortunate abused girls," Jordan said.

Elena nodded and said, "I didn't sleep very well either."

226

"Here's what I'm struggling with. When I became a policeman, I took an oath to uphold the law. If I abandon the case against Pierre, I'm violating that oath. But if I uphold the law, a lot of little girls will never have a chance to lead a somewhat normal life. And if I don't uphold the law, I could be prosecuted and very well might lose my job. I feel like I've been put in a box. It's really a no-win situation."

"I understand what you're saying and yet..."

They stopped the car in front of the Younts' home, carefully making their way around the trash that littered the yard, and did their best to avoid the chickens that were running loose. Jordan knocked on the door. *Monsieur* Yount opened it after a few moments.

"*Mademoiselle, Monsieur,* you have returned. *Madame* Lagne told us that you had discovered the girls in the barn. Are you returning to tell us that we will soon be arrested?"

"No. Please, may we come in? We want to talk to you," Jordan said as the door opened for them.

Madame Yount was in her favorite chair and they could hear the muted sound of the girls' voices coming from the barn. To a casual observer, it would seem like a thoroughly domestic moment. A casual observer didn't know there were little girls from Afghanistan in the barn who had been tortured and abused, that they were scheduled to travel to the United States, and that some of the expenses for their care was being funded by proceeds from art theft.

"What do you want from us?" *Monsieur* Yount asked. "*Madame* Lagne told you everything. What more can we tell you?"

Elena spoke for both of them. "Would it be possible for *Monsieur* Kramer to see the girls? I've told him about them, but if it's not too much trouble, he would like to personally see them."

"*Oui. Madame* Sevy is here today. *Mademoiselle* Johnson, why don't you take *Monsieur* Kramer out to the barn? It is too hard for me to walk."

"*Certainement.* We will be back shortly."

They quickly made their way to the barn and opened the door. "*Madame* Sevy, my name is Elena Johnson and this is Jordan Kramer. I was here the day before yesterday. May we come in?"

"*Oui.* We are in the middle of our daily English class."

Elena stole a glance at Jordan and saw that he was having trouble remaining composed. Even though she knew what to expect, it was still heart-wrenching for her to see these young girls. One could only wonder what kind of monsters would do such despicable things to children. Everywhere Jordan looked he saw shocking remnants of what had happened to the young girls. One girl had a peg-leg. Eyes had been gouged out. All of them were malnourished, and many were very small for their age.

One of the youngest girls, who couldn't have been more than 1 ½ years old, toddled over to Jordan and held her arms up, indicating she wanted to be picked up. A jagged red scar ran from her left eyebrow to her chin.

"Can you believe it?" *Madame* Sevy said, "Her name is Noor. Her father did that to her. He wanted a son, not a daughter, so he slashed her with a butcher knife and when she was only one year old, put her out on the streets. Her mother was killed by him a few months after she gave birth to Noor. All of them have stories just as tragic."

Jordan reached down and picked up the tiny little girl with the red scar running from her eyebrow to her chin. It looked like it might be infected. Elena noticed a bright sheen in his eyes, and knew he was trying not to cry.

They stayed for almost an hour, helping *Madame* by reading to the girls from a few tattered children's books written in English.

"If you will excuse me, I need to fix their lunch and then the little ones need to take an afternoon nap. The older ones get in their beds and rest."

"How do you do their laundry? I haven't seen a washer or a dryer. I noticed there were clothes hanging in the yard when we visited last time. With this many girls, I would think there would be a lot of laundry," Elena said, looking around.

"The other women and I take their clothing home and wash what little they have," *Madame* Sevy said. "We bring groceries for them when we come. Pierre and his employer help with the expenses, but there is very little extra for the girls.

Every time I walk into my home with a large bundle of wash, I am afraid a neighbor will wonder why I have so much laundry when I live alone. I wish we had a washing machine and dryer, but there is no money for that. It's far more important that the girls are well-fed."

"We need to leave now so you can fix them lunch, *Madame*. You have been very kind to let us visit. Thank you. *Bonjour*."

Elena looked back at Jordan who was saying goodbye to the little girl he had been holding. He wiped a tiny teardrop off the little girl's face with his finger and gave her a big hug. When he stood up, he wiped tears from his eyes as well.

As they walked back to the Younts' house, Jordan seemed to be in a state of shock. "My God Elena, it's much worse than you described. They're living like animals. Animals live in barns, not little girls."

They re-entered the house through the back door. "*Monsieur, Mademoiselle*, thank you for allowing me to meet your guests," Jordan said. "You are doing a wonderful thing for these children. Rest assured your secret is safe with us. I wish you well. I do have one question. Why are you doing this?"

They were both quiet for a moment and then *Madame* Yount began to speak. "I am Jewish and was born in Germany. I escaped to France during World War II. After being here in France a few months, I met Giles and we married. My two younger sisters were not so lucky. They were killed by the Germans. When Pierre's employer approached us about helping these Afghan orphan girls, it was as if these young girls replaced my sisters."

"You're a very brave lady. I'm sorry you've had so much tragedy in your life. Thank you for telling us," Jordan said, putting his hand gently on the frail old woman's shoulder. He wondered how Giles managed to button her stark black dress, knowing that *Madame* Yount's impaired vision would make if very difficult for her to do.

Elena pulled an envelope out of her purse and gave it to *Monsieur* Yount. "*Monsieur*, you would honor me if you would allow me to help by providing some money to purchase a washer and dryer. Actually, it may help pay for a few other things as well. Thank you for letting me play a small part in their lives."

As they turned to leave, *Monsieur* Yount put his hands heavily on the arms of his chair and lifted himself out of it as he grabbed his cane. "My son says that he remembers you, but he did not offer you a job. Why did you come here?"

"I talked to your son at the restaurant where I work. Yes, it's true he didn't offer me a job, but I hoped if I could find him he could help me."

"You found us, and then lied to us so you could get a job?" he said incredulously. "And then you offer money for a washer and dryer? I don't understand." His hand shook as he held on to the cane for support and his face reddened.

"I was acting selfishly. I had no idea what was happening here. I am truly sorry. I hope I have not caused you any concern. Again, let me assure you, your secret is safe with both of us. We will tell no one. *Bonjour.*"

They walked through the yard, dodging chickens and rubbish. When they got into the Renault Elena began to sob. As he pulled onto the road, Jordan shook his head as if trying to get rid of the memories of what he had just witnessed. It was surreal, almost as if they had just witnessed some type of horror movie. Jordan was having a hard time making sense of what he had seen.

"That little girl, Noor. I can't believe a father could do that to his child. I'm no closer to deciding whether or not there's a God who would allow such cruelty to be inflicted on those young girls, but what I do know is that the gallery that had the paintings stolen was paid in full for its loss by its insurance company," Jordan said. "I don't think the small business galleries here in France, who didn't know the paintings were stolen, should have to suffer a financial loss. But if the insurance company tries to get the paintings back because it paid the insurance claims, that's exactly what will happen. And from what I've seen, I don't think any of the gallery owners can afford to lose the money they paid Pierre for the paintings."

Elena listened to him, willing the tears coursing down her cheeks to stop. She knew Jordan needed to make his own decision about Pierre, and she tried to understand why this was so difficult for him.

He continued, "I don't see where Pierre personally gained from the theft. It seems the only true victim is the insurance company. God forgive me, but it's pretty common knowledge they have deep pockets."

"Jordan, I don't want to sway you one way or another, but have you ever seen a president of an insurance company who was poor?" she asked.

232

DIANNE HARMAN

"No. And I've been asking myself if I can live with myself if the Younts can no longer provide a safe place for these little Afghan girls."

Elena interrupted him, "I'll never forget those little girls. What a living hell they've endured and their scars... Poor babies."

She looked over at him and could see the anguish he was going through clearly reflected on his face. His hands were white where he gripped the steering wheel. "I don't know what to do," he said, taking a deep breath. "I feel sick to my stomach. My whole life has been about catching bad guys. Even before I became a detective, I was brought up in a house where the law was as important as God. I come from a long line of policemen, and to not uphold the law goes against everything in my life."

"Plus, if anyone finds out that I didn't pursue a criminal and do my best to see him convicted, the police department would fire me. My career and everything I've worked for all these years would be thrown away. My father and the rest of my family would be disgraced because of what I did or actually, didn't do," he said, his voice shaking.

"Jordan, this is a decision only you can make. I'm sorry, but I can't help you. I guess it boils down to what you can live with, because no matter which way you go, you're going to have doubts. By a quirk of fate, events have placed you in a god-awful situation." She reached out and put her hand on his arm. "I'm so sorry you have to go through this."

He was quiet for a long time as he drove and then he began to speak. "For me, it's over. No one needs to know I talked to Pierre and went to the Younts' home. I'll tell Chief

233

Lewis that the trail went cold, and I couldn't find the other paintings. I'll tell him that in my opinion, based on what I've been told, I don't think there's anything more that can be done on this case."

"Jordan, you know my feelings about the little girls, but don't let that sway you. I'll respect whatever your decision is, and I promise you, we will never speak of it again, if what you just said is your choice."

"Right now what I need is a good meal, some wine, and some time to digest all of this. I need to call Pierre and tell him what my decision is. Hopefully, that will be the end of it. By the way, I saw you hand *Monsieur* Yount an envelope. What was in it?" he said, pulling his eyes from the highway to look at her.

"Jordan, I haven't been entirely truthful with you." *Maybe this is the time to tell him everything. Maybe he'd understand. No, this isn't the time. He's worried enough that he might lose his job because he's going to do what's right for the little Afghan girls. He has enough on his mind without my past adding to his problems. Who knows, even though he says he loves me, he might start feeling guilty for not turning me in.*

After a long pause, she continued, "I actually have a substantial amount of money. My husband left me very well off. I keep quite a bit of cash in the cottage in case of an emergency. I put a large amount of it in an envelope this morning when you told me we were going back to see the Younts. I think it will help them feed and clothe the little girls who take refuge there for quite awhile, maybe even long enough that Pierre won't have to commit any more burglaries for some time."

Both of them were quite for the rest of the drive. Jordan was hoping he'd made the right decision and Elena was wondering what the future held for her.

As Jordan drove the car into the driveway of Elena's cottage, in addition to everything they'd seen during the day, each of them was saddened to know that this was the last night they would spend together for some time, perhaps forever.

CHAPTER 36

It was just before dawn; the time of day when the color of the sky changed from the dark blackness of the dead of night, to soft blue, and then to pink, and finally to the vivid blue of a fresh new day. Elena liked to sleep with the louvered windows open, letting the night breeze gently sweep into her bedroom and across her body.

She listened to Jordan's rhythmic breathing and knew he was still sleeping. She gingerly opened one eye. *I need to keep this moment in my mind, this moment of total happiness of just being next to him. I can't let him know how much I'm going to miss him.*

Elena continued to look at him, completely at peace, happier than she'd been in a long, long time. She knew all that was going to change, but for now she was determined to simply be in the moment, this precious and wonderful moment with Jordan.

He stirred and slowly opened his eyes. "Good morning, beautiful. You know, Elena, you kind of remind me of a coyote when you do that. Coyotes are loners and watch things for hours. Yup, I think I'll call you my little coyote from now on. How long have you been watching me?"

"For about half an hour. You don't move much when you sleep. I'll bet you're one of those people who sleeps in one position all night and when you get up the next morning, you only have to make one side of the bed. The sleep of the innocent."

"And you don't sleep that way?" he asked.

"No. I'm afraid I'm a very restless sleeper. I toss. I turn. And then I do it all over again. Always have. When I get up in the morning, I have to tuck in the sheets at the bottom and remake the entire bed."

"Come here little coyote. Let me hold you one last time. You know I'm going to miss you the minute I pull out of the driveway, don't you?"

"Yes. I'd really like to know what you and Chief Lewis decide to do about Pierre. I'll give you my email address. It's a way for us to stay in touch. I promise I won't clog up your email inbox with cute jokes and other silly things, okay?" She smiled, but the tears pooling in her eyes said something entirely different.

"Somehow, it never occurred to me that you would. When I get to California, is there someone I could call for you? Is there something you'd like me to send you?"

"I don't need anything, but I would like you to make a call for me. I was very upset when I left the United States. In fact, I was so upset I didn't even tell my parents I was leaving. I'm sure they've been very worried about me. Would you mind calling them and telling them that you met their daughter in France, and that she's fine? I'll give you their number. They don't live too far from you."

"Of course. I'd be happy to do that. And I'll tell them their daughter is very fine; especially when she's in bed with me!"

Elena laughed and the mood lightened. "We've never discussed families other than that you come from a family of policemen. What about your family?"

"They live on the East Coast and I don't see much of them. My father was a policeman and left my mother when my brother and I were very young. She raised us and then remarried when we left home. Actually, I think she'd been having an affair with my stepfather for a long time. They moved to a Florida retirement community a few years ago. My brother lives in Philadelphia and we see each other every year or so. I can't say I'm particularly close to him. Maybe I've never been particularly close to anyone, but I feel very close to you."

She put her finger on his lips. "No. Don't say anything more that's going to make this any harder than it is. I really don't want you to see me fall apart, and I'm pretty close to it right now. Let's just enjoy one another one more time and then you can be on your way."

In the past few days, the love-making between them had been erotic, joyful and deeply satisfying. This time their sexual mood shifted from being like two hungry people knowing they may never eat again to the bittersweet feeling of two people who have known complete happiness and are trying desperately to make it last. Both of them knew they'd never be satisfied with anyone else. It was a tender and poignant moment.

Two hours later Jordan put the last of his things in his suitcase, took the sheet of paper with her parents' telephone number on it and Elena's email address, and put it in his sling bag. He gave her his card and wrote his personal email address on the back. Then he put his hands on each side of her face and kissed her deeply. "This is not the end, my little coyote. I don't

238

know how or when, but we will be together. That I promise
you."

"Oh, Jordan, I wish it could be. I so wish it could be.
Leave, leave now. *Adieu.*"

He turned, picked up his suitcase and sling bag and
walked through the door. Jordan never looked back. He didn't
want Elena to see the tears in his eyes. She couldn't walk outside
and say goodbye. She was sobbing uncontrollably behind the
door to her cottage which she'd gently closed when Jordan
walked out.

CHAPTER 37

Jordan stopped by the Marseille Police Department, returned the gun they'd loaned him, and continued to the airport. He turned in his rental car, took the shuttle bus back to the airport and went through security. The clock above the arrival/departure screen showed he had about an hour before his plane took off for Paris. Enough time for one last glass of really good Rhône red wine. That was something he definitely was going to miss.

The airport bar was jammed. He couldn't figure out whether it was the tail end of tourist season, or if all of the businessmen were getting a jump on international travel by leaving on Sunday. He was just glad he wasn't in a hurry.

"*Monsieur*, may I get you something to drink?" the pot-bellied bartender asked.

"Yes. I'd like a glass of your best Rhône wine. I've developed a taste for it since I've been in the region."

A few minutes later the genial bartender brought him the Rhône. "If I may say so, *Monsieur*, you look very sad. Would it be caused by an affair of the heart?"

Only the French would think someone was sad because of romance. Even so, he found himself saying, "Yes, I had to leave a lady I've fallen in love with, and I don't know when I'll see her again."

"Ahh, *oui, Monsieur*. That is a reason for sadness. The wine will help and so will time. Affairs of the heart can never be ignored. Excuse me, but the man at the end of the bar is signaling me," he said, turning away from Jordan.

Maybe her parents can tell me why she left California so suddenly after her husband's death. It's really odd that she didn't even tell them she was leaving or where she's currently living.

As his thoughts turned to Pierre, he realized he'd neglected to email the chief for the last couple of days. He slid off the barstool and walked over to a booth that had just become vacant, took his phone out of his sling bag and began typing.

Chief, I'm sorry to be so long in getting back to you, but the trail on Pierre went cold after I located three of the stolen paintings. Evidently the rest of the paintings were sold, and I had no luck finding him or his family. It was kind of like looking for a needle in a haystack. I don't know what you've found out, but I'm ready to let the case go and close the file. From what I understand, even if we locate some more or all of the paintings, it would almost be impossible to get them returned to the United States. I spoke with the Marseille Chief of Police and he told me that French authorities are very reluctant to do anything in cases like this. The gallery owner who bought the painting in St. Victor la Coste is an artist himself with little financial means. If he had to return the painting to the insurance company in California that paid the Laguna Beach art gallery for its loss, it would be a huge hardship on him, and might cause him irreparable financial harm, even bankruptcy. Even if we could locate the others, we'd probably have the same result.

COYOTE IN PROVENCE

The United States can't force the galleries to return the paintings because of international treaties that exist between the two countries. And without Pierre, I think we're finished. I'm leaving Marseille in a few minutes for Paris and then back to Los Angeles. I'll be in the office on Tuesday. Let me know what you've found out on your end.

By the way, I'm attaching a photo to this email of the woman I spoke to you about, Elena Johnson. Would you see if you can find something out about her? I'd appreciate it. I'll talk to you when I get back.

He sat there for a long time, thinking about the last few days. Jordan felt his cell phone vibrate, indicating there was an incoming phone call. He didn't feel like talking, so he waited for voicemail to pick it up and then listened to it.

It was Chief Lewis. "It's the middle of the night, but I got up to go to the bathroom and saw that I had a message. Jordan, you did a very good job. I'm sorry you couldn't find Pierre's family, because we've had no luck on this end as well. We've run into a brick wall.

"Although we've talked to several chefs who know him, and speak of him as being highly gifted, none of them knows who he works for or how to get in touch with him. I think it would be a waste of our time and resources to pursue this case any further. Even if we find him, we have no hard evidence that he's the one who committed the crime. Have a safe trip home, get some rest, and I'll talk to you Tuesday. By the way, your captain called and evidently there was a million dollar theft at a Pre-Columbian gallery on Melrose Avenue. He's glad you're coming back, and said to tell you that the case needs your immediate attention and expertise."

Jordan heard his flight being called and put the phone back in his sling bag. He boarded the plane and was pleased to find that his seat was in the front row of the cabin on both flights, so he could stretch out his legs. He got a book out of his sling bag and put the bag in the compartment above his seat, thinking he'd much rather have Elena next to him, talking to him during the long flight. Books were good companions, but Elena would have been much better.

Well, evidently Chief Lewis isn't going to do anything else on this case. I may be finished with Pierre and the Younts, but I am definitely not finished with Elena. I need to call her parents and go see them as soon as possible.

CHAPTER 38

After Jordan left, Elena cleaned the kitchen, straightened up the house, watered the plants, showered, and dressed for work.

Well, fortunately it's time for me to go back to work. Maybe it'll help ease the pain in my heart. I wonder if I should have told Jordan everything. Maybe he would have understood and decided to stay and live here in Provence with me.

He'll probably learn everything about me from my parents. I never should have given him their number. I wasn't thinking clearly. No one can forgive me for what I did, and particularly a policeman. It's probably just as well. I'll have wonderful memories of our short time together for the rest of my life.

When she finished, she walked down the lane to Henri's Bakery. It was a busy day and it helped keep her mind off of Jordan. When the lunch crowd was gone and it was time for her to leave, she felt lost, at loose ends.

As she was leaving Henri's, she remembered that the wonderful days she'd spent with the man she'd fallen deeply in love with had begun because of an Alfred Mitchell painting on display in the gallery in the village. Although she vaguely remembered the painting, she decided to visit the gallery and look at it again. Jordan had said it was one of the best paintings by Mitchell he'd ever seen.

She hoped the walk would clear her head and she was curious about the Mitchell painting. A few minutes later she spotted it in the window of the Galerie Reynaud. Jordan was right; it was a little jewel. On an impulse, she decided to buy it as a remembrance of Jordan. She opened the door of the gallery, setting off a little bell. *Monsieur* Reynaud came into the gallery from the back room, wiping his hands on the smock he wore.

"*Monsieur,* may I take a look at the painting in the window?"

She examined it and understood what Jordan had been talking about. If he hadn't told her about the frame, she wouldn't have noticed that it seemed much newer than the painting. It looked exactly like the one on the painting at the Younts' home.

"*Monsieur*, what are you asking for this painting?"

"Ahh, *Mademoiselle*, it is an excellent piece by a well-known early California Impressionist, Alfred Mitchell. I am asking 4,500 Euros. I am sure I could get more than that for it, but the tourist season is over and I need some cash to buy some painting supplies. In fact, starting next week I will be closed on Sundays until spring. It's fortunate that I was here today."

"I'm glad you were open. I want to buy the painting. I assume I can pay for it by check?"

"Indeed! My pleasure. You look familiar. Do you live locally?"

"My name is Elena Johnson. I am the luncheon chef at Henri's Bakery. I don't think I've seen you there."

"Ahh, *Mademoiselle*, the pleasure is mine. Your reputation precedes you. Everyone is talking about the wonderful lunches at Henri's. I don't like crowds, but I love to eat! Excuse me. Let me wrap this for you. Would you like me to put it in a bag?"

"Yes, please. I would appreciate it if you could put it in one with handles. *Merci beaucoup.*"

A few minutes later she walked out of the gallery, the remembrance of her time with Jordan in her hand. When she got to the cottage, she hung the painting on the wall behind the couch. Elena spent the rest of the evening looking at it. The painting was beautiful, but it was no substitute for Jordan. She knew she'd wonder for the rest of her life if she'd made the right decision in not telling him about her past.

I can't go back to the United States. I just hope I haven't destroyed another man who loved me. What's wrong with me?

Elena tossed and turned all night in bed, trying to answer her own questions. She woke up the next morning determined to put the past behind her. She hoped cooking would help her forget what might have been.

Suddenly she thought of what she'd discovered on the laptop: the formula for the anti-aging drug; the formula for Freedom; and the formula for the combination pill. Between the discovery of the little girls and Jordan leaving, she'd almost forgotten about it. She decided she'd think what to do about it later.

SOUTHERN CALIFORNIA SEPTEMBER, 2010

CHAPTER 39

Jordan landed at Los Angeles International Airport about 3:00 in the afternoon. After easily clearing U.S. Immigration and Customs, he got on the 405 Freeway south, exiting at Seal Beach Boulevard.

His oceanfront home in Sunset Beach was a much larger house than he needed. Jordan knew he couldn't really justify having a house this big, but it had been a good investment.

One of his pleasures at the end of the day was to sit down with a glass of good wine and watch the sun set over the Pacific Ocean. On clear evenings he could easily make out Catalina Island, just twenty-six miles away. The sunsets were particularly spectacular in the fall, and he never tired of looking at them. It was as if a blazing red fireball was sinking over the horizon.

Jordan was exhausted when he got home and went directly to bed. He didn't even bother to look at the mail his cleaning lady had left for him on the kitchen counter.

Wide awake at 4:00 a.m., he got up, made some coffee, wished he had a French croissant, and began to read his mail. His thoughts kept going back to Elena. He wondered if her parents would be able to meet with him later in the day.

Jordan was at his desk, going through files and papers when his phone rang at 7:30. It was Chief Lewis. "Good morning, Jordan. I hope you had a chance to rest up. I wanted to talk to you before everyone else tries to get your ear and tell you how important their case is and asks for your help."

"Actually, Chief, I slept well last night, but it always takes a couple of days to catch up and there's a lot going on here at the office."

"Is there ever a time when there's not a lot going on at a police station? Anyway, like I explained in my voicemail message, I've decided not to do any more on the Yount case. I think you should call your friends in Laguna Beach and thank them for the tip about the stolen Mitchell painting. Tell them our department can't justify the expense of launching a further investigation into the theft and trying to find the person or persons who stole the paintings. Even if we located Pierre Yount, we still couldn't arrest him for committing the burglary.

"I also want to talk to you about the woman you called Elena. I did a background search on her and learned that her given name is Maria Rodriguez Brooks. Her husband was Jeffrey Brooks."

"Wait," said Jordan, interrupting him. "I know that name. There was something in the papers about him."

"Well, he would have been famous if he'd won the Nobel Prize like everyone said he was going to," the chief said. "Supposedly he gave his beautiful Latina wife, Maria, an anti-aging hormone which was strictly against the policy of his employer, Moore Labs. He was fired. She worked there as well, and was also fired.

"Using his termination pay, they bought a motel in a remote desert area off of Interstate 10 outside of Blythe and fixed it up. No one knows what happened, but Jeffrey was shot and killed at close range with a gun which was never found. Nearby was a knife with Jeffrey's fingerprints all over it."

"Are you sure Elena and Maria are the same woman?"

"Yes, I'm afraid so. Jeffrey's body was discovered by a trucker who routinely stopped at the motel for a cup of coffee. When he got there, Maria was gone. She cleaned out their bank account and left for Marseille. The police tracked her there, but the trail went cold. I believe you've located her. There's a police bulletin on her put out by the detective investigating the death of Jeffrey Brooks. This Elena person is described as a person of interest. I'm not going to do anything with this knowledge, Jordan. If you want to tell the detective who was working the case that you've found her, that's up to you."

Jordan was quite for a long time. *Well, that sure explains a lot.* "Chief, I'd like everything you have on the case."

"Are you sure you want to get involved in this, Jordan?"

"Knowing what I know of Elena/Maria, I can't believe she killed her husband, unless it was in self-defense. She gave me the name of her parents and their phone number. Maybe they know something. I'm going to see this through."

After hanging up the phone, Jordan reached for a new file that had been placed on his desk while he was gone. It was the file for the Pre-Columbian theft that Chief Lewis had mentioned in his voicemail message. It made Jordan wonder if Pierre had made a recent trip to South America. *Will I think about him every time a file comes across my desk? Yeah, I probably will.*

CHAPTER 40

Jordan's day was filled with paperwork regarding his trip to Provence, talking to the hysterical Pre-Columbian gallery owner, interviewing the police officer who was the first one to respond to the silent alarm, and checking to see what was happening with the other cases he'd been working on before he left.

At 4:00 p.m., he picked up the phone and dialed the number Elena had given him. It was answered by a young man with a thick Mexican accent. "May I speak with Mr. or Mrs. Rodriguez?" he asked.

"Yeah, I'll get her. She just got home," the young man said.

A moment later a woman with a soft Mexican accent spoke, "This is Mrs. Rodriguez. Who is this?"

Jordan began to speak, "Mrs. Rodriguez, my name is Jordan Kramer. You don't know me. I've just returned from Provence, France, and I met a woman who told me she's your daughter. She said to tell you she's fine. I have her picture, too. Would it be possible for me to come and speak to you in person?"

There was a long silence on the other end of the phone. He had a sick feeling she wouldn't see him and he'd never know the truth about Elena. Finally, Mrs. Rodriguez spoke, choking back tears. "Mr. Kramer, if what you say is true; this is the happiest day of my life. When can you come? My husband will be home about 6:00. We live in Santa Ana. Let me give you the address."

"Yes, I can be there at 6:00. I'll see you then." The chief had printed and blown up the photo from Jordan's cellphone. Jordan stared at it for a few minutes before putting it into his bag.

He had two sling bags. One had the LAPD logo on it and the other one was the one he had taken to France with no logo. He chose the one with no logo, knowing that people who lived in certain areas of Santa Ana often had a deep-seated fear of the police, particularly when they lived in the barrio. He didn't want the conversation with the Rodriguezes to stop before it even started.

Jordan left police headquarters in downtown Los Angeles and drove south towards Santa Ana. Traffic was heavy as usual. He found the address Elena's mother had given him. It was a small, tired looking house, badly in need of repairs. Paint was peeling off the siding and there were bars on the windows. It reminded him of the Younts' cottage, and he understood why Elena had felt the need to leave money.

As he made his way up the cracked weed-filled walkway to the house, the front door flew open and two young men hurried out. They wore low black shorts, tennis shoes, sunglasses, and had gang tattoos prominently displayed on their arms. Whoever they were, Jordan was glad they weren't going to be present when he talked to Elena's parents.

He pushed the doorbell, but there was no sound. *Must be broken. Better knock in case it is.* The door was immediately opened by a slender, middle-aged, Mexican man. Behind him was a stooped woman with grey hair surrounding her creased face. One look at her was all you needed to know that her life had been one of hard work and disappointment.

"Hello," he said, "I'm Jordan Kramer. You must be Mr. and Mrs. Rodriguez. May I come in?" He had the manila folder with the photograph of Elena/Maria in his hand.

"Yes, please come in," the man said in a tone as soft as his wife's had been on the phone. "I am Fabian Rodriguez and this is my wife, Elena Rodriguez."

My God, she took her mother's name when she left. Her mother has been with her the entire time and her mother never knew it.

He walked into the tiny living room. Babies were playing on the floor and there was clutter everywhere. Silver duct tape covered the holes in the worn upholstery on the couch and chairs. Jordan took the photograph of Elena/Maria out of the envelope and handed it to Elena.

"This is a picture of the woman I know as Elena. I'm certain it's your daughter, Maria. She looks like you," he said to Elena's mother.

As she held the photograph of her daughter in her hand, her eyes filled with tears of happiness. Elena gave it to her husband. "*Madre de Dios*, she is alive. Every morning since she's been gone I have gone to Mass and prayed to the Virgin Mary for her safety," Elena said, asking Jordan to sit down. "Please, tell us everything."

"Mr. Kramer, what has Maria told you?" Fabian asked, carefully putting the photo down on the table, as he sat down on a badly worn grey plaid chair.

"Nothing, absolutely nothing. I wanted her to come back to the United States with me, but she refused. Please, can you tell me what this horrible secret is that she carries? She must have wanted you to tell me or she never would have given me your telephone number."

"I will tell you what we know," Maria's mother began. "Maria married a scientist whose name was Jeffrey Brooks. They seemed happy for several years, but they left Moore Scientific Labs, where they both worked, very suddenly, and bought a motel out in the desert near Blythe. Maria told me Jeffrey had been working too hard and was suffering from burnout. We never went to the motel. Maria would call and tell us what they were doing to fix it up. She said Jeffrey had built a scientific laboratory in the basement where he was conducting experiments.

"For over a year they seemed to be doing fine at the motel, then Maria stopped calling. We tried calling her, but there was no answer. Soon afterwards a police detective came to our house. He told us that Jeffrey had been murdered and that Maria was a person of interest in the investigation of his death. He told us she'd taken their money and run away to France. The police followed her to Marseille, but they couldn't find her."

Fabian interrupted her, "We think that must be where the money comes from." He looked at Jordan. "Maria was very generous with us. She knew we didn't have enough money to feed our growing family. You see, we have many grandchildren who also live with us. Since Maria's been gone a mysterious deposit has been made into our bank account every month. I asked the bank where it was from. They could only tell me it was from some account in a place called the Cayman Islands, wherever that is. We always hoped it came from Maria, because that would mean she was alive. Who else would send us money?" He shrugged his thin stooped shoulders.

Jordan spoke, raising his voice to be heard over the television. "She's still very beautiful and lives in a cottage near a little village in an area of France called Provence. She's become the luncheon chef at a well-respected restaurant in the village. I wanted her to come back to California with me, but she said there were too many memories. She refused to tell me more."

He took a deep breath. "She wanted me to tell you that she's fine and doing well. That's really all. I'll tell her that I've met you, and I'll let you know what she says." As he began to leave, Fabian shook his hand and Elena stood up on her tiptoes to kiss his cheek.

When he got home he went to his computer and composed an email to Maria.

I miss you, my little coyote. You'll be happy to know that Chief Lewis is closing the case against Pierre. I told him that the leads led nowhere and that I couldn't locate the rest of the paintings or find his parents' home. I don't like lying, but I wouldn't have been able to live with myself if I'd done otherwise. He wasn't getting anywhere with the French authorities. Even if we found Pierre, we couldn't actually put him at the scene of the theft. So that part is over. I wish there was something I could do about the children we saw, particularly the little one, Noor, that I held in my arms. I guess the only thing I can do to insure their safety is to do nothing that might cause them to be discovered.

COYOTE IN PROVENCE

Elena, remember when I took a photo of you? Well, I sent it to Chief Lewis to see if there was something I should know about you, since you wouldn't tell me why you didn't want to come back to the United States. Although I've fallen in love with you, I know you are keeping secrets from me. He ran your photo through the U.S. Immigration and Customs Enforcement photo comparison machine and found out you were a person of interest in your husband's murder. He contacted the detective who worked on the case and he doesn't think you'd even be arrested for Jeffrey's death, but if you were, your lawyer could plead self-defense and you would get off.

I met your parents tonight and they send their love. They miss you. I want to live happily ever after with you, and I intend to make that happen. I will do everything in my power to help clear your name. I know you could never do anything like that. I love you. Please, little coyote of mine, come home.

Elena read the email while tears streamed down her cheeks. She was lonelier than she'd ever been in her life. All she could think about was being with Jordan. She stood for a long time, looking at the Mitchell painting and then she walked over to the window. As she looked out the window at the little village below her, she was filled with a deep sense of fear and, at the same time, hope for a new life with Jordan.

Perhaps it was time for the coyote to go home.

PROVENCE, FRANCE NOVEMBER, 2010

CHAPTER 41

The weeks following Jordan's email had been very difficult for Elena. She wanted to go to California and be with him, but she was still afraid she'd be charged with murder and sentenced to prison. One morning she woke up, realizing that not seeing Jordan again was no longer an option. It was time for her to return to California. And in the very back of her mind was a little voice that kept saying, "Maybe you could find a chemist in California who could make the drug for you. You'll probably never find one here."

She'd just finished dressing one morning and was getting ready to walk down to Henri's when her phone rang. *"C'est* Elena."

The woman's voice on the other end of the line began, *"Mademoiselle* Johnson, you don't know me but I would like to meet you. I am Darya Rahimi, the woman who persuaded the Younts to open up their home to the little girls from Afghanistan. They speak very highly of you and I would like to thank you for the financial help you've given them. I'm here in Provence right now, but I'll be flying back to California tomorrow. Is there any chance you could meet me today?"

Well, this is interesting. Pierre's wealthy employer. Yes, I would very much like to meet her.

"I'm just leaving for work, but if you could come to my cottage this afternoon, that would be fine. Will that work with your schedule?"

"Yes. I'll make it work. I have to spend some time at my plant in Marseille, but I can be at your home around three this afternoon."

"Perfect. Let me give you directions. I'm looking forward to meeting you."

Elena put the phone down and stared at it for a moment. *This is someone I never thought I'd meet. Pierre's employer and the woman who's been helping little girls find homes in the United States for the last three years. I wonder what she's like.*

The time she spent working at Henri's passed quickly. Although Monday was usually a slow day for the restaurant, it wasn't on this particular Monday. The regulars felt they could reclaim their tables at lunchtime, having been reluctant to come on the weekends because of the tourists and the crowds. Elena looked at her watch and realized she had just enough time to get home and fix some iced tea before Darya would be arriving.

"*Bon jour*, Henri. I have a guest coming to my cottage to visit me. See you tomorrow."

She quickly walked up the hill to her cottage, changed clothes, and took some cookies out of the freezer. She heard the sound of tires on her gravel driveway. Looking out the window, she saw a shiny black limousine come to a stop in the driveway and a beautiful dark-haired woman got out of it.

Elena opened the door. "Welcome to my home. I'm Elena Johnson," she said as she held out her hand. Darya quickly walked over to her and shook her hand.

"I'm Darya Rahimi. Thank you for taking the time to meet with me."

"Please, come in. I was hoping we could sit on the patio, but the wind has come up and I think it will be more comfortable inside. I see there is a man with you. Would you like to invite him in?"

"No, thank you. It is my bodyguard and he'll stay outside, watching the house."

Elena gestured for Darya to sit on the couch as she placed the iced tea and cookies on the coffee table.

Darya began, "I wanted to meet you and personally thank you for your generous gift. It will go far in helping little girls get from Afghanistan to California. I've been doing this for three years, but the economy has taken a downturn and I don't have the ability to financially help as much as I have in the past."

"May I ask what your business is?" Elena asked, interested in what the woman did that allowed her to have a private jet, a private chef, a limousine service and a bodyguard.

"Yes, I am the owner and founder of Darya Cosmetics. I've always been interested in women and their health, both physical and mental. I know when I feel that I look good, my life seems better and my mental attitude reflects it.

"I have a Doctorate in Chemistry, so rather than spending my life in some boring lab, I decided to devote myself to helping women by developing and selling cosmetics. Now if I could just find some way to make them look like they never aged," she said, smiling, "that product would probably make more money for me and help them more than anything else."

Madre de Dios. Is this a sign? I can almost hear my mother telling me it's a sign from God. Why else would this woman be here?

"Don't you have a lot of chemists working for you? Do you miss doing what you were trained to do? I imagine running a large company takes you from that."

"Yes. I have a lot of chemists working for me, but I personally test every product myself. If my name is going to be on it, I want it to be right, and I trust myself more than anyone else. So yes, I'm still very actively involved in chemistry. After all, every cosmetic is some sort of a chemical compound, nothing more. I know there are cosmetics which are chemical free and organic, but mine aren't. As beautiful as you are, I'm guessing you probably don't buy much make-up."

"Actually, I love to look at make-up. The French drugstores are incredible. I could spend all day there. Let me ask you another question. Do you have manufacturing plants in different countries, and if you do, is there a universal language that chemists use for their formulas, kind of like doctors write in Latin?"

"Yes, there is a universal language for chemistry. It won't mean anything to you, but a chemist can look at any written formula and decipher it. It's complicated and I don't want to bore you with it. But, that's an odd question. Why do you ask?"

"Please excuse me. I'll be back in a moment. I have something I want to show you. Help yourself to another cookie and have some more tea."

When Elena came back into the room, she had a notepad in her hand. "Does this make any sense to you?" she asked, handing Darya the pad on which she'd transcribed Jeffrey's formulas.

Darya bent over the pad and then raised her head and looked at Elena. "These are chemical formulas. Where did you get these?"

"It's a long story. They're mine. They were left to me by my late husband."

"Well," Darya said, "I can tell you what the ingredients are and how much of each ingredient it will take to make the product described in the formula, but there's nothing to indicate what the ultimate product is when the formula instructions are followed. Do you know what type of product is produced?"

"Darya," Elena said, taking a deep breath, "for some reason I trust you. I would ask that anything said here today is not repeated or disclosed to anyone. I have my reasons."

She began to tell Darya the story of how she and Jeffrey had come to buy the Blue Coyote Motel. She went on to describe how Jeffrey had invented the three formulas, slowly gone mad, and eventually how she shot him in self-defense when he attacked her with a knife on that terrible afternoon at the Blue Coyote Motel.

"Darya, the first formula is the anti-aging compound, the second, called Freedom, is the 'feel-good' drug, and the third is a combination of them in pill form. I took the anti-aging hormone and Freedom was piped into all of the rooms in the Blue Coyote Motel. Although I didn't take the pills, I know they worked because people kept buying them. When I was exposed to Freedom, I never had a problem with depression, a condition that had plagued me for years. When I took the hormone, I didn't look like I was aging. It was truly a miracle. I'm telling you this because I want you to know they work.

"I was able to read what the ingredients are and I looked them up. Although they come from South America, they're available in Mexico at certain drug processing factories, but they only ship to bona fide laboratories in the United States. Jeffrey went to Mexico hoping to meet with a company who would be willing to send him what he needed. He was successful and found someone to send him the processed materials."

"Elena, do you have any idea what these formulas could be worth? To have something that would stop people from aging and also make them feel good? You can't put a price on that."

"Darya, I just discovered these formulas a few days ago on a laptop computer that was my husband's. I had a software program on it for the motel bookkeeping and I occasionally used it to search for recipes, but that was about it. I'm as surprised as anyone. He always told me his formulas were in his head. I wonder if on some level he knew he was going insane and decided to write them down. To be perfectly honest, I'd love to have one of those pills now."

"I'm certain I can have them made up for you. Actually, I'd like to think about the two of us going into business together.

We wouldn't be able to sell the pills in the United States, but there's no reason we couldn't sell them from my plant in Mexico.

"People buy my cosmetics to look better. If I could offer them something that would make them feel better and also stop them from aging, they'd be standing in line to get the product. This is huge, Elena, absolutely, unbelievably huge."

"Jeffrey seemed to think it could be when he originally developed it. But after he lost the Nobel Prize and was banished from the scientific community, he didn't want anything to do with the FDA or any other government entity."

"I can understand that, but in Mexico there is very little regulation or supervision. Are you planning on staying here or going back to the United States?"

"Well, I've met a man who wants me to come to California and says he can help me clear my name. He's a police detective. I've fallen in love with him. I couldn't bring myself to tell him about Jeffrey and everything else, but I asked him to call my parents when he returned to California. He did and they told him what the police told them, so now he knows some of my story."

"Elena, let me do this. I have to go to Mexico next week. I'll call my head chemist and see if we can get the plants to make the pills. If we can, I'll try to make them while I'm there. Then, we'll need to talk about what to do next. I don't want lawyers involved at this point, so let me write you a receipt for these three formulas. I'll also write a letter saying that they belong to you and I'm simply carrying out a wish by you to determine if they can be formulated. I'll also state that no one else will have access to these formulas and that I alone will test them. I'll have the driver and my bodyguard witness my signature. Will that be all right?"

"Under the circumstances, I think that's fair and I don't think we can do anything else. I've decided I'm going to go to California, to Jordan. After you leave, I'll make my reservations. I want to spend Christmas with him. That's about a month from now. I'm the luncheon chef at Henri's Bakery and I need to give him plenty of notice so he can find a replacement for me."

"Elena, let me ask you something. If I can make the pill, and I'm sure I can, will you take it?"

Elena paused for several minutes. "Darya, I don't know. I don't want to age and I don't want to be depressed. Does anyone?"

"No, and I might take the pill as well."

DIANNE HARMAN

ACKNOWLEDGMENTS

I want to thank all of people who read *Blue Coyote Motel* and encouraged me to write a sequel to it. The question people always asked was "What happened to Maria?" She was responsible for this book and the soon-to-be published final book of the trilogy, *Coyote Comes Home*, now being written.

As always, I could not have written this without the help of my husband, Tom. He became adept at fixing dinner, doing laundry, and taking care of the garden. Thank you!

And to Michelle, Bernie, Travis, John, Chris, Kirstin, Noelle, Duncan, Marsha, and Jackie, thanks for your support, answering my constant questions, and giving me valuable feedback. Your support and friendship are greatly valued by me.

And to all of you who have read my books and taken the time to contact me and give me your input, please know how very much it's appreciated. None of this would be possible without you. Thank you!

ABOUT DIANNE HARMAN

Dianne lives in Huntington Beach, California with her husband, Tom, a former California State Senator, and her dog, Rebel. She is currently at work on *Coyote Comes Home* as well as the second book in the *Tea Party Teddy* series.

Website: www.DianneHarman.com
Goodreads Author Page: http://ow.ly/mDVP8
Facebook Author Page: AuthorDianneHarman
Twitter Username: @DianneDHarman
Email: dianne@dianneharman.com
Amazon: *Tea Party Teddy* http://amzn.to/ZgKwIB
Amazon: *Blue Coyote Motel* http://amzn.to/SO8uIj

Blue Coyote Motel, an Amazon Kindle Best Seller, was a quarterfinalist in Amazon's Breakthrough Novel Award Contest and was also a Goodreads Psychological Thriller of the Month Book. *Tea Party Teddy* is an Amazon Kindle Best Seller as well.

To keep current on new releases, please go to the email above and just put "Add Me" in the Subject line. Thanks!

www.ingramcontent.com/pod-product-compliance
Lightning Source LLC
Chambersburg PA
CBHW070854250626
47159CB00003B/1059